Roscoe's Revenge

(A Claire Burke Mystery)

by

Emma Pivato

For you, Dave
I think you will
see inside this
guy's mind. No
everyone could!
– Emma Pivato

This book is fiction. All characters, events, and organizations portrayed in this novel are the product of the author's imagination or are used fictitiously. Any resemblance to actual persons—living or dead—is entirely coincidental.

For information, email **Cozy Cat Press**,
cozycatpress@aol.com or visit our website at:
www.cozycatpress.com

ISBN: 978-1-939816-56-6

Printed in the United States of America

Cover design by Paula Ellenberger
http://www.paulaellenberger.com

1 2 3 4 5 6 7 8 9 10

This book is dedicated to the memory of my good friend, Lillian Stover Harvey, 1961-2013. Lillian was born at a time when there was not as much understanding and appreciation of persons with Down Syndrome as there is today. Fortunately for her, she had two older sisters who vigorously fought her school yard battles and parents who advocated tirelessly on her behalf. The result was that Lillian grew up with a good sense of self and a very interesting personality.

Lillian took a special interest in our daughter, Alexis, who she always referred to as “my girl”. She was also fond of my husband, Joe, and the feeling was mutual. However, Lillian and I had a special bond. She was a wonderful friend to me, always very loyal and supportive, but when she felt I was out of line she was not afraid to tell me! One of my most tender memories of Lillian was how she used to gently chide Joe when he would make pointed remarks in my direction: “Joe, Joe…you be nice to my Emma!”

The character of Roscoe in this book was much informed by the many years I was blessed to have Lillian as my friend.

The one other person I must remember on this page is my husband, Joe Pivato, who has always been there for me, every day of our married life, and continues to support me in all of my ventures.

Table of Contents

Chapter 1: A Bad Boss and a Bad Man

Roscoe was angry. He walked stiff-legged to his locker and carefully opened it. He pulled out his backpack and put his lunch inside. He took down the picture of his parents he'd placed on the top shelf of the locker and packed that. He packed his special work cup and the package of emergency Ramen noodles he kept there in case he ever forgot his lunch. He checked to make sure the locker was empty. Then he closed the locker door and placed his padlock in his backpack and hooked his backpack onto his back. "No more" he said. "Me not work here any *more*. Bad lady!" Then he left.

Once outside, Roscoe looked from left to right and for a few moments confusion covered his anger. But then he remembered those early trips with Claire before she'd arranged for him to come to work by DATS (Disabled Adult Transportation System). He could see the Petro Canada Gas Station at the end of the block and remembered that they had passed it on their way here. He walked in that direction. When he reached the corner, he again felt confused but decided to cross the street and keep going in the same direction. Then, on the left, he saw the little café with the alley beside it. That was the way they had come! Roscoe remembered that it was a *long* alley. Roscoe started down it with renewed confidence. Maybe he could remember the route all the way home. Maybe Claire was wrong and he did not need DATS after all!

Roscoe plodded along the alley, fuming over the way Yeung Lan had treated him. "She mean!" he said to himself. "She *bad*!" Suddenly, he heard an odd noise and looked ahead, his view partially blocked by a large dumpster. As he stepped around the dumpster, he saw the source of the noise and reflexively stepped backwards. An older man was shouting at a young guy in his late teens or early twenties. Roscoe had seen both of them before. The younger one had told Roscoe that his name was Sam. He worked in the restaurant clearing tables and sometimes helping out serving customers when the café was really busy. He was always friendly and polite to Roscoe and Roscoe liked him. And Sam was kind to others, too. Roscoe had seen him on several occasions serving an extra-large piece of coconut cream pie to an older lady who came into the café often. He had heard her say that it was her favorite. It was Roscoe's favorite, too, and that was why he'd noticed. Roscoe had also seen Sam talking to the older guy outside the back door of the cafe, sometimes arguing with him. Lately, these conversations had seemed even more unfriendly than usual.

Roscoe stood back in the shadow of the dumpster and listened to this latest argument as it grew more and more violent. Soon the older guy started shoving Sam and it looked like Sam was trying to explain something. Finally, the older guy just threw up his hands in disgust and started to walk away. But suddenly he stopped, pulled out a knife, leaped back at Sam and plunged it ferociously right into his chest. Sam crumpled to the ground and the man leaned down and checked his pulse. Then he backed away, glancing all around him and caught Roscoe's eye. He put his finger to his lips and then ran it across his throat in a menacing gesture before turning and running quickly down the alley.

Roscoe stood stunned, not knowing what to do. Finally, he walked hesitantly towards the body on the ground. "Sam, *Sam.* You okay?" he asked, leaning over and shaking Sam's shoulder. But there was no response and Sam stared back at him with glazed eyes. Roscoe backed away and trembled. He didn't know what to do. Help! He needed help. But who? Not that bad lady! *Claire!* He could call Claire!

With shaking fingers, Roscoe pulled the cell phone Claire had given him out of his pocket. It was a simple flip phone with large numbers. He tried to remember what he was supposed to do. *Number one!* He was supposed to push number one! He pushed the number and held the phone to his ear. Nothing happened. Roscoe felt panic bubbling up in his chest. *Calm!* he thought. *Stay calm!* He repeated the Japanese chant his uncle had taught him several times over. Then he looked at the phone again. "Number one; push talk. Number one; push talk." That was what Claire had told him, again and again, rehearsing it with him every time he came home from his work at the café. Roscoe tried the phone again and this time he heard the ringing sound at the other end. One, two, three rings and then he heard Claire's voice.

"Claih, Claih" he said. "Claih, Claih, you hep me. Need hep. *Need hep!"*

"Roscoe, where are you?"

"Alley. The alley. *Dumser."*

"Roscoe! I'm coming—in the car. You stay on the phone. *Stay on the phone!"*

Claire Burke whirled out of the house and jumped in the car. Into the phone, she said, "The alley where we walked when you first went to work, Roscoe?" Roscoe did not answer.

"Roscoe, that alley—our alley?"

"Yesh, yesh," he finally said, his obvious stress making his articulation even worse than usual.

"I'm coming. *I'm coming. Stay there. Don't move!"*

Three minutes later, Claire wheeled her car into the alley and saw the dumpster ahead. Then she saw Roscoe standing stunned in the middle of the road. She would talk to him another day about safety but not now. Claire jarred the car to a halt, jumped out and ran to him. He reached out to her helplessly, his hands covered in blood. Claire hesitated a second and then threw her arms around him, stroking his back rhythmically.

"It's okay, Roscoe. It's okay. Everything is going to be okay." Claire felt him relaxing a little, and releasing him gently, she walked over to the fallen man. She knelt over him and felt his pulse. Nothing. She pulled out her cell phone and, with shaking fingers, dialed a number she knew too well.

"Sergeant Crombie here."

"Hello, Michael. It's Claire Burke here. I'm afraid I have to report another murder." Claire's voice cracked when she said 'murder' and she suddenly thought it would be very good to be able to sit down.

"Where are you?" he asked, simply.

In the alley beside the Marydale Café at,uh…51st Avenue and 112th street. *Please come!"*

"I'll be there in ten minutes or less—but *he'll* want to come, too."

"I know—but if you're here, I can manage."

"Hang on, Claire. Be right there!" and Sergeant Michael Crombie, staunch ally of Claire Burke, but second in command to Inspector Donald McCoy, hung up the phone.

Chapter 2: Trouble with the Law

Inspector McCoy strutted up in his usual arrogant way, with Sergeant Crombie following faithfully behind. "Where's the body?" he snarled.

Claire pointed mutely to the other side of the dumpster and the two men went over to it, Sergeant Crombie kneeling down to feel for a pulse.

"He's gone," Claire said, weakly.

Inspector McCoy looked down the alley and then back at Roscoe. "Who's *this?*" he demanded.

"Mr. Roscoe Ohura. Roscoe, I would like you to meet Inspector McCoy and Sergeant Crombie," Claire said, falling automatically into her coaching role. As team leader at Roscoe's group home, she was experienced and comfortable with helping Roscoe and his housemates handle experiences out of the routine.

Roscoe smiled tentatively and held out his hand to Inspector McCoy. McCoy did not reciprocate but instead addressed himself to Sergeant Crombie.

"Blood on his hand, Crombie. Check him out." Claire sputtered but McCoy commanded her to stand back.

Sergeant Crombie ambled over to Roscoe in a relaxed manner and addressed him. "Hello, sir. May I check your hands, please?" Roscoe held his hands out mutely and looked at Claire with frightened eyes. She nodded silently and smiled at him. Sergeant Crombie examined Roscoe's hands and the blood on his shirt and then asked him to turn around. He made some notes in his little book and then took some pictures. He looked at McCoy for further directions. McCoy nodded and Crombie proceeded with the interrogation. Claire smiled to herself with satisfaction, thinking, *He knows what a bumbling ass he is in interviewing people with disabilities and is not going to mess it up this time!*

"Sir, are you the person who found the body?" Crombie asked shrewdly.

"I saw. I saw that man. He hurt Sam! Sam *die?*

"Yes, sir. Sam is dead. I'm sorry. Was Sam a friend of yours?"

"Sam good. He nice to me. Sam my friend."

"I'm very sorry for your loss, Roscoe."

Roscoe nodded his head.

After a pause, Sergeant Crombie went on. "Can you tell me what happened this morning, Roscoe?"

Claire nodded appreciatively. Inspector McCoy had not said a word so that must mean that he *was* capable of learning. After the hash he'd made out of interviewing Roscoe's autistic roommate, Bill McKay, during another murder that had occurred recently, he must have realized that interviewing people with disabilities was not his forte.

"Today Tuesday. I go to work. Boss lady not *nice* to me so I quit. She *mean!*" Roscoe looked at Crombie as if waiting for confirmation that he understood. McCoy opened his mouth but Crombie looked at him pleadingly, shaking his head slightly, and McCoy shut it again.

Crombie looked back at Roscoe and nodded his head in agreement. "Some bosses are like that. Very hard to work with. Just no good!" Roscoe nodded his head and Claire could see him relax slightly. But just then there were more sirens and the technical crew arrived, along with the medical examiner. Suddenly, the alley was very busy and Roscoe got that frozen, frightened look again.

Crombie put his arm around Roscoe and said, "Too noisy. Too busy here, now. Roscoe, would you like to go in that café there and have a drink and maybe a piece of pie and we can talk some more?"

Roscoe looked questioningly at Claire, who smiled and nodded in agreement. Sergeant Crombie turned to her and said, "I'll call you on your cell if I need you. Just give us about 15 minutes, please." Then he led Roscoe off without a backward glance at McCoy who was busy instructing the technical crew and getting in the way of the Medical Examiner. But McCoy soon turned his attention back to Claire, demanding that she explain who Roscoe was and tell him what she knew about the situation.

Chapter 3: Claire Gives McCoy the Background

"Roscoe is Bill McKay's roommate at the group home. You remember Bill, don't you?" she asked.

Inspector McCoy nodded his head mutely and Claire thought she saw him wince slightly, which gave her a certain measure of satisfaction. It was evident that he remembered Bill.

"Roscoe was in the Forbes Centre in Calgary with Bill," she continued, "but his parents moved him here from Calgary when they retired. They came here shortly after Bill arrived."

"So they let McKay out?" Claire knew that McCoy was referring to a time a few months earlier when Bill McKay had been accused of murdering a nurse at the Clive Centre. McCoy was the one who'd sent Bill to the Dual Diagnosis unit at Wild Rose Hospital for assessment after accusing him of the murder.

"Oh, Bill's not at Wild Rose anymore," Claire said sweetly. "You remember the judge said he could leave because there was no *real* evidence against him? Well, the problem was that because he'd been *accused of murder*, his care center wouldn't take him back, and no reputable group homes wanted to take a chance on him either. So we bought a house for them across the street from Jimmy and Tia Elves' house. You remember Jimmy and Tia?"

McCoy definitely winced *this* time and Claire concealed a smirk. He was the one who'd accused Jimmy Elves of murdering his wife, resulting in his first major tussle with Claire and his first lost battle with her. Claire went on. "After his wife died, Jimmy brought his disabled sister, Mavis, from the Clive Center to live here in Edmonton. The three families bought a house across the street from Jimmy to use as a group home."

Claire went on. "Tia and Jimmy—they're together now—wanted Mavis, Bill and Roscoe to be close to them. Jimmy is also Bill's co-guardian—and you remember Tia?" This time, McCoy just rolled his eyes, undoubtedly remembering his run-ins with Claire's pesky buddy Tia. Claire noted his continuing silence and smiled. *Hmm*, she thought, *I really am a good teacher*—a fact she was appreciating more and more with the coaching success she was having with Mavis, Bill and Roscoe—an important part of her role as team leader in their community living home, as it was properly called. However, she had avoided using that term with Inspector McCoy, not wanting to lose him completely.

"And Roscoe was here today, why?" McCoy finally asked, with a faint measure of his old assertiveness.

"Roscoe spent twenty years in an institution, so, of course, he hasn't had many learning opportunities. But he's actually quite intelli—"

"If he's so intelligent, why does he talk baby talk and why does he slur all his words?" McCoy asked, falling back into his old habit of interrupting and not allowing Claire to get on with her story.

"You may have noticed by his physical features that he has Down Syndrome?" Claire inquired, not mentioning that on her first meeting with Roscoe, she herself had missed this point, attributing these features to his Asian ancestry.

"Yeah, I've met a couple of Mongoloids before and I wouldn't exactly call them intelligent!" McCoy responded, the ghost of his old, cocky and bigoted side reemerging.

"According to IQ tests, for what they're worth, people with Down Syndrome generally range in intellectual ability from Moderate to Low Average levels of functioning. Bess, the hospital psychologist in the Dual Diagnosis unit at the hospital, assessed Roscoe as falling just below the Low Average range so, relative to the majority of the Down Syndrome population, he's quite intelligent, as I said." After a pause, Claire added "You remember Bess?" Bess had been the psychologist who'd assessed Bill McKay and had seriously undermined the credibility of the murder accusation against him. Claire watched McCoy slyly when she said this and had the satisfaction of seeing him wince again.

"So why does he talk that way, then?" McCoy asked. "Is it because of his big tongue?"

Claire assessed McCoy's tone and wondered if this time he was asking an honest question instead of just throwing out a sneering rejoinder. It *sounded* that way. Maybe there was hope for him yet! She answered his question carefully, anxious not to sound too preachy and risk undermining the tenuous accord that appeared to be developing between them.

"According to what I understand from the literature I have been reading about people with Down Syndrome, it's not because their tongues are too large. It's actually because their jaws are underdeveloped and there's a term for it—micrognathia, meaning small jaw. This causes huge difficulties with articulation, as it would for any of us in the same situation. As a result, their ability to communicate is very limited."

"But that doesn't explain the baby talk!"

"Actually, it does. They struggle every day to be understood and quickly figure out which of their words are the most comprehensible to others and which are just beyond their capacity to articulate in a meaningful manner. The tongue plays an important role in speech and is placed in different locations in the mouth with each different sound. Some of those places are more difficult to position than others and some are just impossible. For example, it's much easier for them to articulate 'me' than 'I.'

"But it sounded like he was just stringing together some nouns and a few basic verbs. It can't be that all pronouns and everything else fall into the harder to pronounce category!"

"No. That's true. But the other thing is hypotonia. People with Down Syndrome have lower muscle tone than average which is why they walk with a broad-based gait and kind of roll from side to side sometimes. That also affects their mouth control. Articulation is a hard task for them and every word is open to misunderstanding, so they tend to keep their speech as short and telegraphic as possible."

"Okay, I get that. But you still haven't told me what he was doing out here this morning."

"I *will* if you give me a chance," Claire responded, a hint of her old asperity in evidence before she caught herself. "As I said earlier, Roscoe has a work placement. Three times a week, he works at a small restaurant a couple of blocks from here. He was hired by the owner, Wu Chen, at minimum wage to clean the bathrooms, wash the floors and load the dishwasher. The promise was that he could gradually work up to some sous-chef work—washing vegetables, fetching implements and materials for the cook and keeping the kitchen organized. Unfortunately, he couldn't handle peeling and chopping safely and efficiently because of his reduced hand strength and finger dexterity which is part of the overall picture of Down Syndrome."

"Go on," McCoy said, with some of his old impatience.

"Well, Mr. Wu had split up with his wife, Yeung Lan, and he and Roscoe got along fine and everything was going smoothly. But then Wu and his wife reconciled and she returned to her old role in the café, mostly accounting and handling the staff. She was horrified to find that her husband had hired somebody with a disability and somebody who was Japanese to boot!" Claire went on, editorializing about the anger many Chinese people held toward the Japanese because of their invasion of China in World War II. Some people could immigrate to this country and leave old rivalries behind, as Wu Chen had done, but others could not—Yeung Lan included. McCoy sighed in frustration at this aside which he considered to be unnecessary, but he said nothing because he, too, it seemed was trying to keep the detente going with Claire.

"Anyway," Claire concluded, things must have come to a head this morning and Roscoe just quit and walked out. I don't have the details yet but I imagine your sergeant is getting them right now. I know that this Sam guy who was murdered worked at Roscoe's restaurant as a busboy and an occasional server and that he was always nice to Roscoe. That's all I know about that." Claire went on speculatively, "Roscoe must have been trying to find his way back home. I had tried to travel train him initially and we walked back and forth to the restaurant via this alley a number of times when he first started his job. However, I never felt he fully understood the route and worried something could go wrong, so I arranged DATS for him even though Roscoe's house is only about five blocks from the restaurant."

"Do you know what time he left the restaurant?"

"No, you'll have to talk to Yeung Lan about that. You know where the restaurant is? Just go back down this alley to the main street and turn right. The restaurant is about two blocks down on the right hand side. You can't miss it. It's called 'The Piccadilly Fish and Chips Shoppe'."

"Wha-a-t? What do *Chinese* people know about running a Fish and Chips shop?"

"You will have to ask *them!"* Claire replied tartly. "My understanding is that they wanted a business in their part of the city and this is what was available here at the time. I believe they *did* keep on the original cooks though."

"I'll go to the restaurant now," McCoy said, and without so much as a good-bye he strode off.

Chapter 4: Roscoe Tells His Story, Not the Whole Story

"How's it going?" Claire asked, addressing herself to Sergeant Michael Crombie, seated with Roscoe in a booth in the café. She glanced sideways at Roscoe as she said this and saw him sheepishly trying to cover the remnants of two separate pieces of pie with a too small napkin. Claire shook her head but said nothing, considering what kind of a day he'd had. She scanned the table and did comment when she saw the small tape recorder in one corner. "You know anything you have on that recorder won't be admissible in court. You needed the consent of his guardian *first*!"

"Ah, Roscoe and I are just getting to know each other," Crombie declared in his soft Scottish brogue. "And I hope you don't mind about the pie. Roscoe couldn't choose between the Field Berry and the Banana Cream so I got him both. He *did* leave some of the crusts, as you can see. I was telling him how fattening crust is."

After a short pause, Sergeant Crombie went on "I wasn't planning to use the tape in court but I was having trouble understanding everything Roscoe said. I thought if I taped our conversation you could help translate and I also thought you needed to know exactly what Roscoe said since there was no guardian here. Right, Roscoe?" he asked, turning to him.

Roscoe, looking full and at least somewhat relaxed, just nodded his head. Obviously, he was feeling comfortable and safe with Sergeant Crombie. Claire smiled at him affectionately and only said, “Back on the diet tomorrow, Roscoe, but it’s okay that you had the pie today.”

Then she turned back to Sergeant Crombie. “What did you learn?”

“Well, I know why Roscoe quit his job when he did and if I’d been him I would have done so, too.” Crombie looked at Roscoe and nodded his head affirmatively before continuing. “As you know, part of Roscoe’s job at the restaurant is to clean the bathrooms. He cleans the women’s washroom before the restaurant opens since it’s obviously difficult for him to go in there after. Roscoe likes to do a thorough job and he had cleaned everything but needed to fetch more paper towels for the dispenser. By the time he found them—apparently they weren’t where they were supposed to be—the restaurant had opened and two girls were in the washroom. I gather they were teenagers by the way he described them. Anyway, he ducked in quickly after they left to put the paper towels in the dispenser before somebody else needed the washroom and then he saw what the girls had done.”

“What?” Claire asked in alarm.

“From what I could gather from Roscoe, and he was pretty upset telling this part of the story so it wasn’t too clear, they had used the toilets and not flushed them and then thrown whole rolls of toilet paper into them. They had scribbled some swear words which Roscoe apparently recognized as such, on the mirror with lipstick and they had smeared soap from the soap dispenser all over the counter.”

“Oh, that’s terrible!” Claire exclaimed, her stomach churning with anger, and she looked at Roscoe sympathetically. “What happened then?”

“Roscoe just dumped the towels on the counter and ran out after the girls. He caught up to them just when they were leaving and stood in front of them blocking the door. From what I could gather, he scolded them for what they had done and demanded that they go back and clean up the mess."

Claire grinned at Roscoe, nodded her head up and down vigorously and holding up both thumbs! "So what happened then?"

"Apparently, the wife of the owner came over and bawled Roscoe out for talking to customers that way. Roscoe tried to explain what they'd done but he was upset and couldn't get the words out so she could understand. Meanwhile, as far as I can understand from what he told me, she was telling him this was a serious misbehavior on his part and if he ever treated a customer that way again he would be fired. The girls were just standing there smirking at him and then they flounced out of the store and were gone. Roscoe then told the woman that he was quitting, cleaned out his locker and left."

"And she didn't try to stop him?" Claire asked, through gritted teeth.

"Apparently not. Roscoe did not say so, anyway."

"Roscoe?" Claire turned to him.

Roscoe had been listening all this time but seemed content with the way Sergeant Crombie was telling the story and apparently didn't feel the need to add anything. Now he just shook his head and said, "She not say anything to me, not even gu-bye!"

"I'll report her!" Claire hissed. "She *knew* you weren't supposed to travel unsupervised. Something could have happened to you. Something *did* happen and you could have been *killed!* That man who killed your friend, did he see you?"

But at this, Roscoe just put his head down and said nothing.

Crombie explained, "I've asked him about what happened in that alley several times, but he won't say anything. It's as if he's blocked it out. We just don't know—and if the man *did* see him, he could be in danger, too!"

"I'm going to take him home now. I assume you have no objection?" she asked challengingly.

"No. *I'll* deal with McCoy. If he's talked to the café owner, he'll have the timeline now and have to realize that there was a logical reason for Roscoe to be in the alley when he was. And the tape will help."

"I want a copy," Claire said. "I might understand something you missed."

"Don't worry. I plan to get you a copy. I already thought of that possibility."

Chapter 5: Trauma and Memory Tricks

Claire's first task when she and Roscoe arrived back at the home was to contact his parents. They needed to be updated on what had happened to him that day. Claire agreed to meet them at her home later that evening as she had to be back there by 3:30 when Jessie returned from school. Jessie was Claire's and her husband Dan's 12-year-old daughter who'd been born with multiple disabilities including athetoid quadriplegia, cortical blindness and a severe seizure disorder. Dan worked from home much of the time and Claire worked there, too, part-time with her interior decorating business. The couple's flexible work schedules, along with some limited government help for caregiver assistance for Jessie had made it possible for them to carry on a reasonably normal lifestyle, despite Jessie's severe disabilities. But tumultuous events of the last few months, including the sudden urgent need to create a home for three disabled adults who'd previously been in an institution, had taken Claire in a radically new direction, and she was now a 'team leader' for the new home, responsible for making this brave new situation work.

Before leaving Roscoe's home for the day, she sat down with him at the kitchen table quietly and tried to get him to tell her what had happened in the alley and who had stabbed Sam. However, Roscoe just put his head down and moaned. And when she pressed him further he just covered his ears and rocked back and forth chanting, "No more Sam; No more Sam; No more Sam." Finally, Claire gave up.

Claire was not one to give up permanently, though, and the next day she tackled the other part of the issue: his former job. Roscoe was adamant that he did not want to return to the restaurant, but Claire was just as adamant that he needed to go back one last time to talk it through with Yeung Lan. She insisted that Roscoe needed and deserved an apology from Yeung Lan and he was going to get it. Claire telephoned to arrange a meeting time and they were able to meet that very morning. When she and Roscoe arrived, they discovered that Wu Chen was also there and he insisted on sitting in on the meeting despite Yeung Lan's concerns over who would manage the restaurant. Claire suspected that this was just a cover-up for her larger concern which was that her husband might hear Roscoe's version of what had happened.

"Sally is here and she can handle the front alone for a while. The lunch crowd won't be in for another hour," Chen responded, and sat down firmly at a table with the group.

Claire, then asked Roscoe to tell the story of what happened before he quit. Roscoe looked fearfully from one person to the other, but Claire kept urging him and finally he began to talk, keeping his eyes focused on Wu Chen. However, Yeung Lan kept interrupting Roscoe, claiming that she didn't understand what he was saying, and Claire was obliged to keep translating. This actually turned out to be a good thing, though, because the constant reviewing of what he'd just said helped to keep Roscoe on track so he could produce a more coherent story.

When Roscoe described the things the two girls had done just after he'd cleaned the washroom, Wu Chen snorted in disgust. He turned to Roscoe and said, "I am sorry this happened to you. Just wait until the next time they try to come into my restaurant. I will tell them they are not welcome, that they are banned for life. I can do that and if they file a complaint, I have something to show any inspector who comes." He pulled out pictures he'd taken and explained that he'd arrived just after Roscoe left. On hearing the story, he had inspected the bathroom and seen the mess.

"Who cleaned it up?" Claire asked.

"My wife had to do that. I was busy," he replied, shortly, and Claire suspected that a longer story was involved. She hid a smirk, relishing the poetic justice of it.

Wu Chen had been shocked to hear that Sam had been killed and that Roscoe had witnessed the actual killing. Turning to him, he asked, "Who did it, Roscoe? Have you seen him before?" But he got no more response from Roscoe than Claire or Sergeant Crombie had managed. He asked Roscoe to please consider coming back, telling him he was a good worker and they valued his contribution. His wife started to object, but Wu Chen just glared at her and she remained silent. However, she need not have worried, because Roscoe made it quite clear he was never coming back.

Wu Chen then turned to Claire, expecting her to support his request, but she just said, "Roscoe is an adult and it's up to him." Then to soften this and not burn any bridges because she really did like Wu Chen and it had been a good placement for Roscoe, she told him that if Roscoe ever changed his mind, she'd let him know immediately. "I know he was initially very happy here and really liked working for *you,"* she stressed, looking directly at Chen.

They left then. Roscoe said a polite 'good-bye' to Mr. Wu and shook his hand, but he ignored Yeung Lan entirely. They returned to the group house then, and it was time for Claire to face her new problem. It was not right for Roscoe to be sitting around home every day.

Chapter 6: Roscoe Finds a New Interest

Claire did not think a day program, like the one she'd found for Bill and Mavis, was appropriate for Roscoe. Yet he continued to act fearful and unwilling to consider a new job or even to work with Claire in exploring the possibilities that might be available. By the end of the week, they were both looking and acting a bit stir-crazy. Claire had pretty much used up her store of ideas to keep him busy: games, reading, spelling and math exercises, walks, shopping and house cleaning together, and visits with Claire's Aunt Gus and her new friend, Amanda, who lived together in Amanda's house across the street.

Roscoe had more or less cooperated with all of these activities, but Claire could see his heart wasn't in it and he continued to act nervous and preoccupied. She had tried several more times to get him to describe who he'd seen in the alley with Sam, but his response was always just to clam up and then become even less involved in whatever they were doing together at the time.

Finally, in desperation, Claire arranged an evening meeting with Roscoe's parents and Tia and Jimmy Elves at her home to brainstorm ideas that might possibly help bring Roscoe out of his shell. She was feeling desperate and had even asked Amanda and Aunt Gus to join them.

It would have been more convenient to hold the meeting at the Elves's home because Jimmy and Tia were obliged to bring along Tia's nine-year-old son

Mario, on a school night. Also, if the meeting had been at the Elves's, it would have been easier for Roscoe's parents—Fuji and Yuna—to pop across the street to see their son, and for Amanda and Gus—older ladies in their mid-seventies—to not have to travel at night, since they lived next door to Jimmy and Tia. However Dan, Claire's husband, was away on a business trip and so she had to be home with Jessie. Jessie did have an assistant with her until nine, but Claire was afraid the meeting might last longer.

That evening, at eight, after they were all settled in Claire's living room and Jessie was in her bedroom doing range of motion exercises on her bed with her assistant, prior to retiring for the night, Claire explained again the reason for the meeting and suggested that they all just put their ideas on the table, but not comment on them until everyone had had a chance to speak. Mario was sitting on a chair beside them in the living room enjoying the rare privilege of playing computer games on Tia's iPad. He had not been invited to join them at the table.

Fuji started. "Yuna and I could take Roscoe on a road trip, maybe to Vancouver." Vancouver in February did not sound very good to Claire, but she just said *O-o-kay.*

Aunt Gus, never one to follow the rules, blurted out "How would that help? He'd just be running away from his problem temporarily, not solving it!"

Claire gave Gus a warning glance and reminded them all, "No comments until everyone has had a turn!"

Amanda offered, "How about taking him to the Yellowbird Casino? Lots of lights and action and it gets really exciting when somebody wins. Maybe he'd like it, and it would help him forget his troubles and maybe he could even get a job there!"

"Perhaps," Claire replied noncommittally. "Anybody else?"

"Umm—" Yuna spoke up, clearing her throat nervously. "Roscoe has always been interested in food and cooking. That's why he liked that job at the restaurant so much. He told me that he was hoping some day they would let him help out in the kitchen. Maybe we could start up a little restaurant, ourselves," she said, looking at her husband. "I know Daisuke would really like that and want to get involved—and Roscoe would feel comfortable working for *us.*"

"Wow! That would be quite an undertaking!" Claire could not help saying—and Fuji nodded his head in agreement, implying that it was somewhat of a pipe dream.

"Excuse me," young Mario piped up from his near-by chair. "Are you people familiar with 'The East Wind Rising Art Centre'?"

Nobody said anything. Mario continued. "Well, when Jim-Dad and I were at the Edmonton Art Gallery recently to see a performance art exhibition, we also saw a smaller display of work from artists from that centre. I had a chance to talk to the director and she told me it's a centre for people with cognitive disabilities who are interested in art. Roscoe's interested in art, isn't he?"

Mario didn't wait for an answer, but went on. "Well, she told me that you can either take courses there or just drop in any afternoon a week. All you have to pay is $2.00 a session to cover the cost of materials. They get a city grant for their salaries. Anyway, I bet *that's* something Roscoe would like to do. I know he likes to draw. He showed me some of his pictures once. I think he's pretty good! And maybe after he was there for a while, he'd get to feeling really comfortable and then maybe he'd draw a picture of that man in the alley!"

Tia blushed because she was not sure she should have told Mario about Roscoe. But Mario acted so much like an adult that sometimes she got confused and shared information that normally should stay just between adults. Nobody said anything at first, the usual reaction to the adult speeches that often sprang forth full-grown from his child's mouth. But then Claire, who knew Mario better than anyone else there except his mother and perhaps Jimmy at this point, spoke up enthusiastically, breaking her own rule. "It might work. It might just work! *Thank you,* Mario!"

A couple of other half-hearted suggestions followed but most of those present gravitated to Mario's idea and it was finally agreed that Claire should put Mario's suggestion to Roscoe and try to meet with the director at the Centre as soon as possible. Jimmy smirked and Tia rolled her eyes. Mario just went on playing his computer game as fast as he could while he had the chance! It wasn't often that his mother indulged him in this activity.

Chapter 7: Claire Tries

The next morning, Claire got in touch with Sarah Hughes, the East Wind Rising Centre Director, and arranged an appointment for that very afternoon. Only after that was settled did she approach Roscoe about it, reasoning she could always cancel if absolutely necessary but that he would be more likely to agree if the wheels were already in motion. At first, he stated that he was not interested, but Claire persisted.

"Look," she said in exasperation. "We can't just sit around here in the house every day like a couple of lumps. Everybody needs to do *something* with their lives. You *know* you have some artistic talent, Roscoe. Maybe with a little more practice you can turn it into a work opportunity—design posters or illustrate children's books or *something!"*

Roscoe said nothing in response, but Claire continued on, speaking firmly. "Roscoe, we're going to meet with that lady and look at her art school and meet some of the other student artists. If nothing else, it will get us out of the house for the day. If after that you're still not interested, then we'll forget it. But there's no sense turning your nose up at something until you know what it's about!" Roscoe just shrugged his shoulders and left the room, but he didn't object any further.

They didn't arrive at the Centre until two that afternoon—after Claire had concocted a casserole for supper and after Roscoe had finished his shower, his very *leisurely* shower. Sarah Hughes greeted them at the door. She was a vivacious, red-headed woman of uncertain age wearing a collection of brightly-colored garments and scarves. As it happened, there were only three aspiring artists there that afternoon—a young woman Claire guessed to be in her mid-twenties who also had Down Syndrome and two slightly older guys who clearly had some developmental disabilities but no obvious diagnoses.

All three greeted Roscoe with shy smiles and then immediately went back to work on their respective paintings. Sarah asked Roscoe if he'd like to try, and when he gave a weak nod of affirmation, she led him over to a quiet corner richly stocked with paint and crayons and large sheets of paper hooked onto an easel. She then led Claire to the opposite end of the room where a small table was set up with a teapot and cups and ringed by some comfortable chairs. Clearly, this was the staff corner and the two of them sat down to have a chat.

Sarah explained what they were hoping to accomplish for people with disabilities at the Centre. She mentioned some of their successes in the five years that the Centre had been open. These included the art exhibit that Jimmy and Mario had seen, as well as a recent commission to develop cover pictures for three new, locally-produced elementary school readers! Then it was Claire's turn to tell Sarah a little bit about Roscoe and the trauma he'd recently suffered.

"Art therapy is good for dealing with trauma," Sarah said soberly. "Especially for people who, for whatever reason, cannot express themselves well."

"I hope it works," Claire said simply. The remainder of their conversation was spent working out a possible arrangement for Roscoe if Claire could convince him to come back to the Centre. Sarah suggested that they just keep the schedule open. She said Roscoe was welcome to come in any afternoon a week between two and four, and he could come as often as he liked. The same flat $2.00 charge would apply. If he should get really interested after a while and want to take lessons, they could talk about those arrangements then.

Claire thanked Sarah and walked over to Roscoe to let him know it was time to leave. She looked in shock at three drawings he'd produced. All of them were in strong strokes of purple and black crayon despite the rainbow of paints and pencils and other colors available. The first was a very small, tight drawing of a tiny house with two barred windows and a big, solid looking door. There was no walkway leading up to it and no front step. Claire also noted that there was no chimney in the very heavy-looking roof.

The second was a little larger and perhaps the crayon strokes were not quite as heavy. It looked like a group of tightly intertwined trees all in black with heavy branches with purple raindrops falling all around. There was no sun. Right in the middle of the wood was a tiny little horizontal shape, perhaps meant to be a baby, also in purple.

The third and last one looked like the outline of a person standing sideways so his or her face was in profile. There were few details except for heavy black shoes and extra big hands.

"I see you've been busy, Roscoe!" Claire said lightly. "Did you enjoy having a chance to draw again?" Roscoe said nothing. He turned toward his drawings and it was clear he was planning to crumple them up but Claire stopped him. "Could I have these drawings if you don't want them, Roscoe? I could show them to Bill and maybe then he'd like to come here, too," she improvised. Roscoe shrugged his shoulders but said nothing. He walked towards the door where his coat was hanging.

Claire carefully rolled up the paintings and turned away from Roscoe to conceal a satisfied smile. She would show them to Bess, the hospital psychologist who'd worked with Bill and had since agreed to be involved in an advisory capacity for his new home. Claire wanted to see what Roscoe's drawings might tell an expert about his state of mind.

"What did you do today?" Anna asked Roscoe when they returned to the house. Anna was one of the afternoon staff on duty that day. Claire looked at Roscoe but didn't say anything. She had carefully avoided talking to him about his time at the Art Centre or asking whether or not he liked it. Somehow, instinctively, she knew this was the right thing to do because she was seen as "the boss" in the group home and he might feel obliged to please her with a positive answer.

"Claire and I go to aht school," he replied, laconically.

"Oh. And what was *that* like?"

"Go-o-od," he said, and offered nothing more.

Claire intervened at that moment. "Hey, Roscoe. I think it might be time to wash up for supper. I'm leaving now and I'll see you tomorrow. Okay?"

"Bye, Claire," he said, and headed towards the bathroom.

Chapter 8: Claire gets Crafty

The next day, Claire again said nothing to Roscoe about the Art Centre, but she had arranged a trip to the Edmonton Art Gallery and accompanied him there on DATS. She could just as easily have driven him there in her car but she wanted to get him involved again with DATS preparatory to resuming some sort of structured day program. They looked at the performance art exhibition first—the one Mario had mentioned. In a large room a number of boxes were arranged, apparently haphazardly. Pieces of newspaper were crumpled up here and there, some inside the boxes, some half out of them and some on the floor. Cookie crumbs trailed from the corners of some of the boxes and the whole exhibit was simply labelled "Urban Sprawl."

"Somebody made a mess," Roscoe commented. "*That* not right!"

"H-m-mn," was all Claire said about it. "Let's go see something else, okay?" She took him next to the second exhibit Mario had mentioned, the one from the Centre. He looked at a grouping of eleven paintings and drawings on one wall, all mounted in simple, plastic frames from the Dollar Store.

"Oh, look!" Claire said. "Remember that girl we met yesterday at the Centre? Well, that's *her* name on this drawing."

Roscoe said nothing but studied the drawing closely. It was a happy picture of two children having a tea party at a little table set up under an apple tree full of red apples. The sky was blue and a big sun was shining brightly. Then he commented, "That nice. If I see that girl again, I tell her I like her picture."

Claire thought of saying something bright and encouraging to that response, but instead she just kept looking at the rest of the grouping of eleven pictures. "What do you think of this one?" she asked Roscoe. She was pointing at a simple picture depicting an almost leafless tree growing out of a bare ground represented by only a simple line.

"*That* not good!" Roscoe responded. "*I* draw *better!*"

"Well, I'm sure you *can,*" Claire responded. But she couldn't resist adding, "But one thing we can give him credit for. At least he *tried!*"

Roscoe said nothing and soon they wandered off to see other displays in the gallery. Then they went to the cafeteria area to eat the lunch Claire had packed plus a piece of pie Claire purchased for Roscoe, just to make it a pleasant experience in his mind. Soon it was time to wait at the door for the DATS pick-up.

Claire and Roscoe spent the next day at the house focusing on some math exercises, a kitchen cupboard cleaning project, and preparing the vegetables for supper. In the afternoon they took a short walk, retracing the steps they'd originally taken to the café where Roscoe had worked. Roscoe didn't want to go in but Claire saw through the window that coconut cream pie was written up on the daily menu. She suggested they go in and have some. After a short inner battle with himself, Roscoe agreed.

Roscoe looked fearfully around as he entered, but was then greeted warmly by his old friend, Mr. Wu, who led them to a corner table. A friendly server soon came over to take their order and Roscoe relaxed. He hinted that some cocoa would be good with the pie but that was too much for Claire who was anxious to keep Roscoe's weight down and he settled for a bottle of diet Pepsi.

The next morning, after Bill and Mavis had gone off to their day program, Claire asked Roscoe what he would like to do that day. "I thought we could focus a little more on reading today, maybe work through another chapter from your book about Tim, the Avenger. Then we could do some more spelling practice, maybe make it through the next quiz in your book. This afternoon we can start to do some clean-up work in the yard. The snow is mostly gone now. What do you think, Roscoe?"

Roscoe looked at her glumly but said nothing.

"Well, do you have a better idea?" Claire asked.

Roscoe thought for a minute and then asked, "Could we go back to the Ahrt Centre today?"

"I guess,' Claire said nonchalantly. "If that's what you'd like to *do.*" Meanwhile, she was mentally patting herself on the shoulder.

Chapter 9: Roscoe Has Another Scare

In the following weeks, Roscoe fell into a regular habit of attending the Art Centre three afternoons a week. The director was often around and she would examine the works of the various artists throughout the day. She complimented Roscoe on some of his efforts and offered a few pointers on how he could improve them further still. Roscoe gradually began relating to some of the other artists who came there. Different students dropped in at different times, but he generally saw the same half dozen or so at least once each week. The girl he had met the first day seemed to come more often in the afternoons and he saw her at least twice a week and sometimes on all the three days he was there. He learned that her name was Desiree and they often sat together at snack time.

Once Roscoe had settled on attending the Art Centre three times a week, Claire turned it into a regular Monday, Wednesday, Friday routine so she could set up a different activity for the other two days. Claire got him started in an exercise class once a week at a local gym within walking distance and she hoped to gradually raise it to twice a week. But so far, Roscoe was not willing to commit to that. Thus, they still had one day a week open.

On one empty Tuesday, Claire suggested that they go visit Roscoe's former boss at the café. He had been very welcoming the last time they'd gone there and Claire felt it was wise to keep up the connection in order to keep Roscoe's social network as large as possible. Roscoe did not object although he also did not seem particularly enthusiastic. Claire speculated that he still feared a possible confrontation with Yeung Lan, but said nothing.

When they arrived at the café, Roscoe peeked through the window to see if coconut cream pie was on the menu, but suddenly he leaped back and turned away. "Not go there today, Claire. I go home now!"—and he started walking away at a faster pace than his usual, more leisurely speed.

Claire said nothing but went along with him. It was clear that something he'd seen had upset him. Claire had talked to Bess several times since Roscoe had witnessed Sam's murder and was beginning to understand more and more what post traumatic stress disorder could do to a person. Reasoning with Roscoe would be pointless right now she knew, so she just said brightly, "*I* know what we can do this afternoon. We can bake some coconut oatmeal cookies for lunches this week. Would you like to help me do that, Roscoe?"

Roscoe nodded his head but in an absent-minded manner. He looked back over his shoulder and hurried along the street. When they got to the corner, he relaxed a little and gently moved Claire to the inside of the sidewalk, because he knew a gentleman is supposed to walk on the outside. They crossed the street and soon reached their alley short-cut where they turned in.

After another minute, Claire became aware that a car had turned into the alley as well and when it did not pass them she got a funny feeling up the back of her neck. She struggled to be reasonable, but then said to herself, *Don't fight your instincts.* They were far enough into the alley to not be readily seen from the street and she saw the dumpster up ahead. The car was still idling a short distance behind her. As they approached it, she suddenly saw what could happen and grabbed Roscoe by the elbow.

"*Run!*" she commanded and, hauling him along beside her, she ran around the dumpster with him and in behind it. Just then there was a loud crash and the dumpster lurched toward them, but wedged angle-wise against the back of the building before the end of it could reach them. The car sped off just as the back door of the little café flew open.

"What happened here?" a man yelled at them.

Claire had her arm around Roscoe who was shaking violently. "A car tried to hit us! Please call the police!"

The man turned back to grab a phone and a woman came out and took Roscoe by his free arm. "Come in and sit down," she said simply, and Claire gratefully accepted. Claire was trembling, herself at that point and she turned to Roscoe. "What's going on, Roscoe? *Tell* me. You saw something at that restaurant, didn't you? And then that car followed us. *Who* did you see?"

But Roscoe could not answer her. His teeth were chattering at this point and the kind woman slid a cup of not too hot cocoa in front of him with a spoon. He clasped the cup with both hands and drank half of it in one gulp. Food was always the go-to comfort place for Roscoe, and Claire smiled at the woman gratefully. Claire left him alone until he finished his cocoa and then asked him shrewdly, "Who are you afraid of, Roscoe?"

"Sam *dead!*" he said, rocking back and forth. "Sam *dead.* Poor Sam!"

Just then, Inspector McCoy walked in. Claire groaned audibly. Did he not have anything better to do but always turn up in their lives at the worst possible moments!

Chapter 10: Strange Bedfellows

"You!" he said.

"My sentiments exactly!" Claire replied dryly.

"What happened?" he asked simply. *Something was happening to McCoy,* Claire thought. He didn't seem to have his old energy for sarcasm.

"A car deliberately tried to hit us. I think the driver was aiming at Roscoe here." Roscoe had been temporarily distracted by the kind woman offering him a second cup of cocoa, but he turned when he heard his name.

McCoy addressed him directly then. "Young man, please tell me what happened." Claire noted McCoy's surprising attempt at being respectful even though, she suspected, Roscoe was probably older than he was. McCoy had always referred to Bill as a boy when he was working on *his* case.

"Cah! Cah try to hu't us. W-h-y?"

"Did you see the driver?"

"Sam! Poor Sam. Sam *dead.*"

"Was the driver the man who killed Sam, Roscoe?" Claire asked. McCoy glared at her but said nothing.

"Not tell. W-h-y? *I* not tell."

"*Was* he the man who killed Sam, Roscoe?" McCoy asked, with his best effort at being patient and reasonable. But Roscoe did not answer. McCoy turned to Claire. "Did *you* see him?"

"No," Claire responded. "I was walking on the inside."

McCoy raised his eyebrows and Roscoe looked at him and then said, "The lady has to walk on the inside––to keep her safe. You okay, Claih?"

"I'm okay, Roscoe. Thank you for looking after me," Claire said soberly. Inspector McCoy looked like he wanted to say something but then stopped. *Maybe he really was learning something*, Claire thought.

With a sudden, uncharacteristic burst of intuition, McCoy turned to Roscoe then and said, "Roscoe, we have lots of pictures of bad people who hurt others down at the police station. If you come with me and look at the pictures, you might see the driver. You would not have to say anything. You could just point to him. Then we could catch him and he wouldn't be able to hurt anybody else. Would you like to do that to help me catch him?"

Roscoe just shook his head and said nothing. Then he started chanting again and Claire saw the tears in his eyes. "Poor Sam. Sam *dead!* Sam *dead!"*

"I have to take him home now," Claire said firmly. "If you need to question him further you can come to the house tomorrow. Please let me know beforehand so I can arrange for his parents to be there. They are his guardians."

McCoy did not argue but replied he would get one of the policemen on the scene to drive them home. Claire thanked him and they left.

When they got back to the house, Claire asked Roscoe how he was feeling and if he wanted to talk but he said nothing. She turned the TV on and sat Roscoe down in front of a Disney movie called *Finding Nemo.* Then Claire went into the kitchen to quietly tell the afternoon staff what had happened and to warn them not to press Roscoe, but to listen carefully to anything he had to say about the day's events. After these two matters were taken care of, Claire went across the street to see Tia and collapsed at her table.

Tia fed her coffee and her homemade apple cake which happened to be Claire's favorite and then asked "What made you run when you did, Claire?"

"I don't know. I just felt it in the back of my neck somehow. There was something funny about the way Roscoe rushed away from the restaurant after looking inside and about the way that car was driving so slowly down the alley behind us. I guess I was thinking he might try to shoot us and we should hide behind the dumpster. I thought maybe I could bang on the backdoor of the restaurant—I remembered there was a door there—and they'd let us in and then we'd be safe. I never thought he'd try to *ram* us," she said shakily.

Tia gave her a hug and asked her if she'd like to lie down for a while, but Claire suddenly looked at her watch and exclaimed, "Oh, no! Dan's at the corporate office for a meeting and I don't know if our assistant was able to pick up Jessie on time!"

Tia quickly connected to Claire's home number on speed dial and handed her the phone. The assistant Josephine was there and told her Jessie was fine. She was just about to eat supper. Claire thanked her and said she'd be home presently.

After she hung up the phone, Claire said to Tia, "You know Josephine has never let me down once yet and she's only been with us three months. I can hardly believe it after all we went through with Aimée!" Tia just curled her lip in disgust and reminded Claire once more that she should have gotten rid of Aimée long before she did!

Chapter 11: Battle Plan and False Confidence

Needless to say, when Claire told Roscoe's parents what had happened that day, they were *very* upset. Yuna's first thought was to pick up Roscoe immediately and bring him home with them until they could make other arrangements—maybe get him into that institution where Bill had been and where Tia had worked.

Claire winced. This would place their whole staff funding arrangement in jeopardy and also the house itself since Roscoe was part-owner. But quite apart from that, she worried what it would do to Roscoe. Before Sam's murder, he'd been making progress, coming out of his shell and gaining some much needed independence. He'd been treated well at the Forbes Centre in Calgary but everything had been done for him. Now he was learning new skills and enjoying new experiences. Claire did not want him to lose all that.

Fuji interrupted her thoughts. "Maybe that's a bit drastic, Yuna. What about if we pick him up tomorrow and take that road trip to Vancouver? Tom has room for us and he told me before he'd be happy to have us stay with him and Edie for a couple of weeks. Maybe by that time, the police will have found Sam's killer and Roscoe will be safe staying in the house."

Yuna was silent for a moment. She, too, was beginning to appreciate what it would mean for the home they had all worked so hard to establish. She remembered the long hours Fuji and Daisuke had put into getting it ready—and all the planning, and the excitement and satisfaction they'd all felt over making it happen. She thought sadly that she had not felt so close to others since leaving Japan thirty years ago. She had friends now, people with whom she shared a powerful common bond. She turned to her husband Fuji. "Do you think if we worked really hard we could be ready to leave by tomorrow morning?"

"You get the clothes ready and I'll get the van ready. We can do it!"

"What about Roscoe? Maybe he should come back to Randy's place with us tonight."

Claire intervened then. "I really think that Roscoe is safe right now. Whoever that person is, I don't see how he can know where Roscoe lives. And I'll stay and make sure his clothes are all clean and packed and that he has some art supplies and other materials to keep him busy on his trip."

Fuji turned to Yuna and said gently, "I really think that is best. We'll have enough to do getting ourselves ready and there's no place for him to sleep at Randy's. Why don't we do it that way, Yuna?" She agreed grudgingly and Claire went off to tell Roscoe about his trip and to get him ready for it.

At 10:10 a.m. the next morning, which was a Saturday, Fuji rang the front doorbell while Yuna waited in the loaded van with the engine running, ready to go. Claire had been there since eight to make sure everything went smoothly and she handed Fuji Roscoe's suitcase and gave Roscoe his backpack to keep with him in the van as it was full of his art supplies, reading and study materials and the new mini iPad he'd received from his parents for his birthday, already loaded with lots of games. Claire thought wryly that there was a good chance everything else in the backpack but the iPad was redundant and would receive little if any use.

Everyone marched outside to say good-bye to Roscoe. Tia and Jimmy had joined them and Jimmy had wheeled Mavis out as well. Gus and Amanda hurried over to say hello to Yuna and Fuji and good-bye to Roscoe and just generally be part of the excitement. Amanda was wearing her usual comfortable old lady blue velour pants and top, but Gus, as always when in the public eye was dressed to the nines, her sharply tailored black slacks covering an apparently svelte body which Claire suspected was receiving much assistance from Gus's new Spanx bodysuit.

"Bye, Roscoe! See you soon," Bill yelled.

"In two weeks!" Gus said, bossily, addressing her remarks to both Roscoe and Bill.

Roscoe looked back out of the window and waved good-bye—but suddenly his smile froze and he stared hard at a black car idling near-by. Claire caught his look and followed it just in time to see the car pull away from the curb across the street from the house and take off. A chill went down her spine. Of course!

The man who'd attacked them in the alley would have known that if they were walking that they had to live near-by. As Mavis had accompanied them on a couple of their visits to Chen's store, all the man had to do was cruise around the neighborhood and look for wheelchair ramps! Had he heard Aunt Gus helpfully belting out the timeline? It seemed likely since his window was open. Claire went back inside, feeling sick to her stomach, made some staffing changes to accommodate for Roscoe's absence and then went across the street to Tia's house for some TLC and advice.

Chapter 12: What a Crock!

Tia was happy to see Claire but also wanted to spend some precious time with Jimmy since they'd both been very busy lately. Thus, she wasn't quite as welcoming as usual. Jimmy, on the other hand, *definitely* did not look welcoming. Tia briskly cut a piece of apple cake and poured her a cup of coffee and they sat down at the kitchen table together.

"What about yours?" Claire asked.

"I just finished breakfast before Roscoe left."

"That's what I want to talk to you about," Claire said, and told her what she saw. Tia was shocked and suddenly became much more available.

"I'm convinced Roscoe knows who killed Sam but he won't say. It must be somebody he's seen at the café there," Claire said. "Do you think it would be a good idea for us to ask Wu Chen? He seems like a really nice guy."

"What if he's in on whatever is going on?" Tia asked. "There must be a reason Sam was killed and I doubt that it was a crime of passion. Therefore, there are likely illegal activities involved. Maybe Sam knew something and was blackmailing him."

"I don't know. Wu Chen has been really nice to Roscoe," Claire replied stubbornly.

"How about this?" Tia suggested. "Is there anything you need from his café? Some Sesame Oil, maybe?" The basic menu in the café was a variety of deep fried fish with chips supplemented by a few side dishes and deserts supplied ready-prepared by wholesalers. But their special claim to fame was the "high quality" sunflower and sesame oils they used to deep fry their fish. As an extra service, they sold these oils in smaller containers to customers wanting to purchase them.

"We could go over there and buy some," Tia continued, "and if he's there, just visit for a while and tell him what happened in the alley and just see how he responds. That might tell us whether or not we can trust him."

"I don't know now," Claire responded. "We could be setting Roscoe up and leading him like a lamb to the slaughter." Tia rolled her eyes. There went Claire with her clichés again. But Claire went on, speaking soberly. "It's one thing for us to take some of the chances we've taken—"

"You mean *I've* taken, don't you?" Tia interjected, referring back to some of Claire's past schemes which had placed Tia in the line of fire.

"Okay, *fine,* but you *did* have a choice. Roscoe won't even know what's going on."

"Look, Claire, I really can't spend much time hashing this around this morning. Jimmy and I have plans. Let's just walk over to the store and play it by ear. We'll just see how he reacts to us mentioning the attempt on Roscoe's life, but we won't say that we think Roscoe knows anything. Then tonight we can talk about it. Okay?"

It was agreed and they set off. Tia provided Claire with a reusable shopping bag so she wouldn't have to go back to the house to get one. Claire thought about saying that they *did* have plastic bags there but one look at Tia's face told her she better not! Once they arrived, through the front window they could see Yeung Lan at the till and Wu Chen shelving new bottles of sunflower oil near the back.

Tia was about to push the door open when Claire grabbed her elbow and pulled her back and off to the side, out of view of the window. "Wait!" she hissed. "Did you see that sign in the window? They're looking for a cleaner two afternoons a week from 3 to 6!"

Tia turned to Claire with a frosty look on her face. "And that's significant, why?"

"Don't you see?" Claire asked excitedly. "You could take the job and say you could only work evenings and then you'd have time to check around when nobody else is there to see if anything funny is going on! I'm not satisfied," she went on, "that it's just a coincidence that Sam was killed so close to the cafe. What if that woman is involved and that's why she was so nasty to Roscoe?"

"And what am I supposed to do with my son while I clean up yet another person's mess in order to accommodate your grand plans, Claire?" Tia asked sarcastically and with a hint of bitterness in her voice.

Claire hung her head, remembering the disastrous results of Tia's last cleaning/spy mission, but then she said, "I think this would be different. Just keep all the lights on and lock the door. I noticed there are chimes on it so you'd always have warning if the owner was trying to get in. And they wouldn't dare to try anything given so much visibility from the front. And Mario can sleep over at our place and we'll get him to school the next day. You could just drop him off on your way to the cafe or even have him come directly from school on those days and I could help him with his homework." Claire thought she'd better make some return gesture of commitment if she wanted to get Tia on side—and besides, she really liked Mario.

Tia looked at her quizzically and Claire took an uneasy breath. At least that was better than the usual baleful look she got when she suggested a new work prospect to Tia. But then the atmosphere changed. Tia raised her eyebrows in that way she had and Claire braced herself to plead her case.

"Look!" she began.

But Tia just said, "I don't need you to explain it to me. I can see the point. I just don't know if Jimmy will ever agree after what happened at the Clive Centre." Tia was alluding to an earlier adventure which had led her into considerable risk and grief.

"Why does he have to agree? You aren't married yet!"

"And that's no way to *get* married—or *stay* married."

"But what *else* can we do? I don't see any other leads to follow up at this point."

"I know," Tia sighed. "I'll think about it."

"Great! So why don't you go in there and find out what it's all about. I can't do it because they've met me."

"Is that what you call 'thinking about it'?" Tia asked dryly.

"Well, you wouldn't have to make a commitment—and somebody else might apply!"

Tia grinned indulgently at this latest example of her friend's chronic impulsivity.

"I suppose I could do that," she said slowly, all the time wondering what Jimmy would say.

Chapter 13: Into the Frying Pan—or the Deep Fryer

Tia composed herself and entered the store while Claire lurked around the corner, trying to catch a glimpse of the action in the window while still staying well out of sight. Tia approached the counter hesitantly and addressed Yeung Lan. "I would like some more information about the job you are advertising," she said.

"You vacuum, clean bathrooms, wash floors, maybe clean stove...whatever," the woman replied laconically.

"What equipment do you have?"

"You come with me," she said and got up from her chair.

Tia followed her and observed the rather grubby and well-used vacuum cleaner and the grey-mildewed-smelling mop. Logically, she knew that her only reason for taking this job—if she did take it—was to search for some clues to Sam's killer but psychologically she knew that she could not do the kind of sloppy job that such equipment would only allow.

"If I take the job, may I bring my own equipment? I'm used to working with it."

"You clean. I don't care with what as long as you do the job."

Tia talked some more about the hours, explaining she had a son and would have to work those nights when she could get a babysitter in for him.

"We close at five every afternoon and we are usually gone by seven. We are not open Sundays if you want to come then."

"No, I need to spend Sundays with my son. I could come in a couple of nights during the week but it may not be the same nights all the time."

"Okay. That's fine. You take the job?"

"I'll discuss it with my fiancée and my son and get back to you this afternoon. May I see the kitchen now? That would probably be the biggest part of the job."

When Tia saw the kitchen, she quickly composed her face into a rigid mask. There was an overall sense of greyness—grey walls, grey windows and most of all a grey ceiling, merging into a dark brown patch directly above the stove. The stove itself, a huge, black cast iron beast, had been gentled into a dusky grey by many layers of grease. Grease also hung in the air and Tia automatically took shallow breaths. When Tia could trust herself to speak in a neutral tone, she commented "I suppose I would start with the kitchen?"

"No—bathrooms. You make sure you clean the parts clients see first! Then, if there is time, you can clean stove top."

Tia said nothing but she wondered to herself, *Do all Chinese people feel that way about hygiene when serving the public?* She could hear her son's response to such a statement in her head. 'Mom, you're stereotyping. That's what bigots do!' *But there must be some reason so many people comment about the hygiene in Chinese restaurants,* she thought. On the other hand, she'd heard plenty of her parent's Italian friends comment about the hygiene, or lack thereof, in Canadian homes. And who knew what went on in the kitchens of fast food restaurants staffed by disgruntled teenagers!

"Well, do you want the job or not?" Yeung Lan's harsh voice interrupted Tia's reverie.

"I'll call you in a couple of hours," Tia said, and she left.

Chapter 14: Tia Does Her Best

Tia had taken the job, despite Jimmy's vociferous objections. She could see no other way to move ahead with finding the killer and that was that. It was 9:30 the next evening and she'd just finished unloading her cleaning supplies at the cafe. These supplies included new gloves, brushes and cleaning cloths that she'd bought that afternoon, since Mario had gone to Claire's house after school and Tia had had extra time.

She started in the bathrooms, using a toilet brush with a disposable head to get off most of the yellow stains inside the toilets in both washrooms and then going back over them with a new head to finish the job. Tia had sprayed a tough cleaning solution around their bases before that and now went over those areas with the remains of the second brush head to remove the brown stains. This use of disposable cleaning materials affronted her ecological sensibilities but she could not imagine recycling materials that had touched all that filth. Tia was sure that when Roscoe had been in charge of bathroom cleaning he'd done his best but you needed to be an expert to tackle a job like this.

Tia next scrubbed the walls and the toilet surfaces with disposable toweling and the sinks and mirrors with more toweling. She cleaned the walls around the sinks and doors, the light switches and the door knobs with more cleaning solution and toweling and last of all cleaned the floors. All this she managed to do in an hour and after that she threw away her gloves and mask, thoroughly scrubbed her hands and arms and sat down to have some tea from her thermos and the sandwich that she'd brought along with her.

Tia noted wryly to herself that she no longer could or would work fiendishly for hours without a break. Maybe she was getting old—or maybe, with her newfound happiness in her relationship with Jimmy, she no longer had the compulsion to prove herself through marathon housekeeping bouts.

Tia sat in the kitchen and gazed around it in a calculating manner as she sipped her tea, but when she was ready to work again she dutifully went about vacuuming and washing the floors in the rest of the store. She looked at the windows and noted that they could really use a wash but thought she'd leave them for another day since they had not been mentioned by Yeung Lan. It was now 10:30 and with what time and energy she had left she turned to the big job—the kitchen.

Where to start? *Obviously, with the main source of all this dirt,* she thought. She looked closely at the stove and commercial vent above it, so saturated with grease that it dripped slowly back on the stove—and probably into whatever was cooking on it. Tia removed the filter and coated it with a strong, grease cutting solution before placing it in the large commercial sink. She sprayed the same solution into all the inner vent parts she could reach and then cleaned the main ones with paper towels and the tiny coils with q-tips. She found an empty oil bottle in the closet and drained the grease pit into it. By this time, she was able to tackle the filter with a tough brush and more cleaning solution, after which she cleaned it thoroughly in hot, soapy water before reinstalling it. By the time she finished, the stove was once more the shiny black monster it had been initially and it stood in stark contrast to the rest of the kitchen. Tia hastily scoured the sink and mopped the floor and then, finding it was 12:30 on her watch, called it a day.

Only when she'd repacked the car with all her supplies and sat down behind the wheel, did Tia remember that she had not pursued the original goal of taking this job, that is to check around for any clues as to what might have happened to Sam. She was not looking forward to describing this non-progress to Claire. Oh, well. As she'd explained to Claire before, it was necessary to first establish her credibility and build trust with her employer before she could start actively snooping.

Three nights later, on a Friday evening, Tia was back in the store. This time, the vacuuming, floor scrubbing and bathroom cleaning went much more quickly and by 10 o'clock, she was done with all that and had even cleaned the inside of the front windows. After a quick break, she turned her attention back to the kitchen doing what she should have done first of all if she'd not been so obsessed by the stove.

With a special brush mop, frequently rinsed and dipped in strong cleaning solution, Tia scrubbed back and forth across the ceiling, gradually dislodging what she suspected to be decades of grime. Then, standing on the step-ladder she'd brought with her, armed with yards of clean toweling and hopping up and down to move the ladder, she scrubbed back and forth across the ceiling until her neck ached and her shoulders throbbed. But when she finally finished, she noted with satisfaction that the ceiling was white once more. She dumped the used cloths in the garbage, her normal thrift and ecological sensibilities still smothered by an overall sense of repugnance and a strong desire to have no reminders of what had been there when she'd first entered that kitchen.

It was now 11:30 and this time she remembered her purpose for being there. After quickly cleaning the kitchen sink, already well soiled from the three days of frying that had taken place since her last visit, Tia turned her attention to the pantry. During her previous visit she had noticed an oddity—another bottle that appeared to have the bottom cut out of it thrust into a corner. But it was no longer there. Tia remembered being told that the garbage and recycle were picked up Thursday mornings so that was probably why it was gone. She did find one scrap of plastic in the corner though—and it appeared to have some odd white powder on it that definitely was not oil residue. She would show it to Claire and see what she had to say.

Tia looked through the kitchen drawers but there was nothing of interest and no other place to look in the kitchen. She checked quickly and furtively behind the cash register, knowing she wouldn't be able to justify her presence there if one of the Wus came in, unlikely as that was in the middle of the night. It was now 12:30 a.m. She knew that they emptied the till each night. Mrs. Wu had been careful to tell her that. But Tia expected to find some records—bills, receipts, phone numbers, or memos. However, there was nothing. It was as if this was not an actual, functioning cafe and that, in itself, made her suspicious.

In the next two weeks, Tia continued her efforts, cleaning a little more each night she was there. She gradually cleaned walls, doors, light fixtures, shelf surfaces, the fridge, freezer, microwave and, perhaps, most challenging of all, a dish rack for pots that appeared to have years of encrusted grease in the corners. One day, she surprised the Wus by coming at four so she'd have enough light in the short Alberta winter day, to clean all the outside glass. By the time she completed this task to her satisfaction, it was six p.m. and the café was closing for the evening. Chen and Lan were preparing to leave.

Tia had sensed, on the few occasions when she came in early enough to see the Wus before they left, that Yeung Lan wanted to say something to her, and now she came out with it. Would Tia consider cleaning her private home as well? Tia explained that her schedule was quite full. She would see if she could arrange something but would not promise.

It was that very evening, a Tuesday after they were gone, that Tia found what she'd been looking for, the severed parts of another empty bottle. This time she examined them closely, noting that there had been oil in the top part but more of that white powder residue in the bottom. She put the parts in a plastic bag and moved them to the trunk of her car before continuing her cleaning efforts.

Tia was focusing tonight on the pantry—a long, narrow room leading off the wall of the kitchen opposite the stove. She braced herself, expecting to find bugs, perhaps even cockroaches, when she delved deeply into its interior, given what a lovely environment had been provided for them. However, there were none—and then she found out why. The remains of several cans of strong insecticide were lined up along the back wall of the pantry, right next to a large bag of breading mix.

Tia could smell the insecticide from the residue on the top of the tins and just shook her head in disgust. It was time to go home and she decided she was not all that anxious to clean and reorganize the pantry after all. It was not as if she could throw out the packages of various foods and condiments on which she had already noticed an expired date and she did not feel like breathing in that insecticide.

When Tia turned to leave, she stumbled over a large box full of heavy plastic oil jugs that had been parked in the middle of the floor. It was open and she saw that one of the jugs was missing right from the middle of it. She wondered idly why whoever had removed it had not started systematically from one end of the box or the other.

She glanced at the outside of the box and noted with a start that the *M* she had seen on the outside of the broken plastic bottle now in her trunk was the same *M* on the outside of this box. The company name read as Sol de Mérrida and in smaller print the explanation 'aceite de girasol.' *Sunflower oil!* Tia exclaimed to herself. It was very similar to the Italian—'olio di semi di girasole.' Although why 'aceite' should mean 'oil' in Spanish, she did not know. 'Aceto' meant vinegar in Italian. *Ah, the vagaries of languages* she thought. *What a fascinating topic!*

Tia studied the printing on the box further and noted that it included an address: Calle 49, Calle 7, no. 62—near the Ring Road 281. She squatted on her heels and methodically pulled out one semi-transparent plastic bottle after another to examine them, but it was clear that they all contained oil and only oil.

She carried one out to her car and compared it to the broken one in her trunk. They were identical in size, shape and color but the broken one had the extra layer inside, just below where the top part had been roughly cut off. The plastic was an opaque white and when Tia put the two pieces together she saw that the line of division could not be seen from the outside. Tia returned the full bottle to the shop, closed the pantry door and all the lights and left for the night. She never noticed the woman two doors down, standing in the window of her second floor suite, watching her.

Chapter 15: Finally, a Clue!

Claire had been excited by Tia's find and had immediately taken the first plastic fragment to the friend who'd helped her identify a package of strange white substance that she'd had found during their first adventure together. When Tia gave her the pieces of the broken jug, Claire passed those on as well and within two weeks they had their answer. The substance on both surfaces was cocaine! There could no longer be any doubt that the Wus were involved in something illegal. But how did that tie into Sam's murder, if, in fact, it did?

That evening, Claire and Tia met together at Claire's home. Dan was still away so Claire was obliged to remain home with Jessie, but this also provided the opportunity for Claire and Tia to discuss the case without either Dan or Jimmy within hearing distance. Claire started by asking rhetorically, "What do we know, what do we almost know and what do we suspect?"

"We know that illegal activities are happening in the café since we found the evidence of cocaine—and we know that considerable effort has been made to conceal it because of the nature of the bottles—and we know there's an international connection," Tia responded.

"Yes, and we also know that Roscoe witnessed Sam's murder and that somebody tried to kill him. We strongly suspect that he recognized the killer in the cafe and that it was the killer who was in the car that came after him and rammed us," Claire added.

"And we also have strong reason to believe that the killer now knows where Roscoe lives and that he's been stalking him," Tia went on.

"So where do we go from here?" Claire asked simply.

"We could tell all this to Inspector McCoy," Tia offered half-heartedly.

Claire shook her head. "We don't have enough. But how can we get more?"

"I suppose I could take Yeung Lan up on her housecleaning offer."

"No. I don't think so," Claire responded

Tia looked surprised. "Why? You're usually so anxious for me to take advantage of any opportunity to snoop!"

Claire didn't respond right away. Finally, she said, "Somebody tried to kill us. Somebody is stalking Roscoe. The Wu house is either a dead end or it's very dangerous. In either case, I don't want you to go there. There *must* be another way."

"The only other lead we have is the Mexico connection," Tia offered.

"I *know* that!" Claire responded. "I'm *thinking!*" Claire got up to get them more coffee but then asked Tia if she'd like a glass of wine instead.

"Maybe," Tia replied. "I'm feeling pretty frustrated and pretty scared!"

Claire and Tia talked of other things for a bit while they enjoyed their wine. Then Tia thought of something. "Megan's estate is finally getting settled. The lawyer called Jimmy yesterday and apparently the tax matters have now been straightened out so the assets should be released in a couple of weeks."

"I thought that had all been settled long ago. You told me Jimmy used Megan's money to help pay for Mavis' care when she first moved up to Edmonton."

"That was money he found hidden in the house after Megan died. Jimmy didn't declare it because he didn't want it tied up in the estate since he needed it for Mavis. Besides, he was feeling so hurt and angry and betrayed at that point that he wasn't in a particularly upright and honorable mood."

"Well, what about the estate? That's what you started to tell me."

"Megan had bought a house. You know she was planning to move to Mexico?"

"What part of Mexico?"

"Playa del Carmen."

"Which is?"

"Yucatan peninsula, south of Cancun. It's called the Mayan Riviera."

"But the police know she was dealing in drugs. Didn't they consider that was one of the drug assets?"

"No. She did inherit some money from her parents and it was invested there. Maybe she added to it with drug money but they have no way to prove it. Basically, nobody knows."

"Okay. It's nice that you and Jimmy have a house in Mexico but what are you going to do with it?"

"We need to go there and look after it. Up to this time it's been in the hands of a property manager but now that the asset is being turned over to Jimmy, that arrangement is about to expire and there will be nobody to look after it."

"Surely you can renegotiate that arrangement long distance."

"I guess—but Jimmy doesn't trust them. He wants to see what he has and make sure it is safe—decide whether he wants to hang onto it or sell it. Apparently it's quite a large property—and right on the water. It should be easy to sell but he doesn't want to get cheated out of part of what it's worth. He's still determined to get some payback for everything Megan put him through."

"Okay, I can understand that. When are you and Jimmy thinking of going?"

"Well, I was thinking..." Claire raised her eyebrows at this. "You're not the only one who can think, Claire!" Tia continued.

"Well, *what* then?"

"If Jimmy does decide to sell it, we might never have the chance again."

"*What* chance?" Claire asked in an exasperated tone of voice.

"You know how you're always talking about community living for people with developmental disabilities? And normalization and optimizing opportunities and pushing the boundaries? I thought I could convince Jimmy that this was our big chance to give Roscoe and Bill and Mavis a *real* holiday, an escape from the Edmonton winter like so many others enjoy!"

"So you think we should haul them all down to Mexico, to a house we've never seen in a town we've never seen? And...?"

"I've checked it out. Playa del Carmen is a safe part of Mexico—and there are lots of interesting things to do in that area. And *also,*" Tia added triumphantly, "it's not that far from Mérrida. Maybe you and I could take a day trip there if we went down."

"And how would we explain that?"

"Well, I'm sure we'd both be working hard to look after Roscoe, Bill and Mavis—especially Mavis. And we'd need to take a couple of staff down with us. So we could just say that one day we needed a break and wanted to go on a little tour."

"To see Mérrida—which is, of course, the tour centre of Mexico," Claire said sarcastically. "And why would he want you to go off on a day's jaunt with me instead of him?"

"Well, we could say he better stay behind with the male assistant in case there was trouble with the guys."

"Possibly," Claire mused, "but I'm not sure Dan would agree to me going down. He'd have the whole responsibility for Jessie then."

"As you do every time he goes away on a business trip or to a conference. Can't you argue that it's your turn? And it's not as if you don't have good help for Jessie now!"

"But a holiday is different than a conference."

"I don't think we even need to look at it that way. Giving the three of them a real holiday *is* our real agenda. The other is just a side issue, just in case we can find out something…since otherwise we really are at a dead end."

"That's true," Claire said soberly. But it will be a miracle if we can pull it off."

"That's where you come in, Claire. You're good with miracles—and finagling!"

Chapter 16: Roscoe Enjoys His Family Trip

All the way down Highway 2 out of Edmonton, Roscoe kept looking back to see if any black cars were behind them. Sometimes there was a black car and then he would get upset. His dad, Fuji, would patiently explain over and over that there were lots of black cars on the road because black was a very popular colour. Fuji knew there was no point in telling Roscoe not to worry, though. Instead, he said to Roscoe, "You have to watch it and see if it always follows us or if it passes. If it passes, then it's not interested in us." Then Fuji would slow down a little and the black car would pass them. Half an hour and ten black cars later, Roscoe was finally able to accept that they were not being followed and he began to relax.

The rest of the trip was uneventful and Roscoe gradually became more and more like his old, happy self. They stopped overnight in Calgary and went to the zoo at St. George's Island Park. It was not as grand as it once had been before the devastating 2013 flood but there was still much to see. Roscoe took it all in with big eyes. There were so many animals he'd never seen before.

Yuna and Fuji looked at each other sadly and each knew what the other was thinking. Roscoe had been born shortly after they emigrated to Calgary from Japan. They were insecure, frightened and trying to get a foothold in their new country of origin, often working 12 to 14 hours a day just to survive. By the time Roscoe was three, they knew they could not cope with his special needs plus the needs of their two older boys, so they made the decision to place him first in a foster home and later in an institution.

At least in the institution they'd been able to visit him as often as they wanted and had always maintained a very close relationship, but now they felt the full weight of all he had not experienced because of this choice. Fuji took Yuna's hands and said to her softly, "We can't change the past. We can only do whatever we can now to make up for it." Yuna nodded her head mutely in agreement.

After their morning visit to the zoo, Fuji and Yuna and Roscoe carried on down the road to Banff and booked in overnight at the Elkhorn Lodge, a charming, rustic inn at the southern end of Banff with the mountains on grand display all around them. This had not been their plan. Their plan had been simply a visit with their older son and his family in Vancouver and getting there as quickly and expeditiously as possible. However, after seeing how much Roscoe enjoyed the zoo and suddenly realizing how limited his opportunities to know the world around him had been up to this point, they agreed that they needed to change their focus, even if that meant prolonging their trip and spending significantly more than they'd planned on.

This was not a decision they talked through together. Both of them just knew—and both of them silently thanked Claire for opening up the world to Roscoe and helping them to see beyond his disability to who he really was as a person. Roscoe, himself, was enthralled by the quaint rooms, the looming mountains, the huge trees and the birds flitting between them. At least for now, it was clear that his recent trauma was tucked away in a safe place allowing him to experience the present unburdened.

The next morning, they drove to Lake Louise and hiked up the mountain as far as Mirror Lake. More than that seemed too much for all of them and they returned to the magnificent Chateau Lake Louise where they treated themselves to a bountiful lunch. After that, they carried on down the road to Field, B. C. where they stayed again in a quaint cabin and were fortunate enough to see a train entering one of the impressive spiral tunnels carved through the solid mountains that made the Canadian coast to coast train system possible.

The next day, they got up early and drove straight through to Vancouver, or more specifically, North Burnaby where their son and his wife and two daughters lived in a modest split-level. Benjiro, his wife, Hinata, and their daughters, Miko and Momo, ages 8 and 10, respectively, were all happy to see them. The girls were rather taken aback by Roscoe at first, but gradually they began to understand his slurred speech and soon they had him involved in a Wii game of tennis. Roscoe could not keep up with their fast moves but he didn't mind losing and seemed to enjoy the action.

The next ten days passed quickly with a variety of activities. Roscoe was enchanted by Stanley Park, continuously gazing in awe at the huge trees. He was a little leery of the Seaplane Tour, especially when it splashed down in the water and when they returned home he had a big bowl of ice cream and a long nap to offset it.

What really frightened Roscoe, however, was the Capilano Suspension Bridge. Despite all of his brother's urging, he could not bring himself to travel more than a few feet on it. The continuous swaying of the bridge terrified him in a way that the rest of them could not understand since they did not know what it was like to live in a body with low muscle tone and poor proprioception. That is to say, Roscoe could not orient himself in space very effectively so on the swaying bridge he felt completely out of control. Yuna and Fuji realized sadly that there was much they did not know about their son. They wondered if in the time they had left on this earth they could ever recoup that loss.

The last day of their visit ended on a high note. They spent the entire day in downtown Vancouver, hopping on and off the city tour bus, and eating a delicious seafood lunch at a cozy restaurant near the wharf that specialized in fish less than two hours out of the sea. Roscoe tasted oysters for the first time, gulping and wincing as they slipped down his throat but still appreciating the taste. Tia would have approved his choice of Spaghetti alla Vongole and he also tasted some of his brother's dish of mussels in white wine.

That evening, like many evenings before, Fuji and Yuna sat at the kitchen table with Benjiro and Hinata after the children and Roscoe had gone to bed, talking about everything, but always coming back to the subject of Roscoe, his new life and the current threat hanging over him. Fuji had phoned Claire and found out that the perpetrator was still at large but Claire took the opportunity to suggest to Fuji a new plan of action. He mulled it over in his head but did not share it with Yuna just yet. He knew how over-protective she could be.

Chapter 17: Claire Proposes a New Adventure

Almost immediately after Roscoe and his family returned to Edmonton, Tia and Claire arranged a family meeting to discuss their recent idea. On a Tuesday evening, Claire, Jimmy, Tia, Fuji, Fuji's brother, Daisuke, Yuna, Bill's aunt and guardian Marion, Gus and Amanda met in Tia's and Jimmy's living room where tea, de-caf coffee and cake (a nutmeg, sour cream cake with coconut icing) were served by Tia, as pre-arranged, while Claire ran the meeting.

Claire began. "We are all aware of the threat to Roscoe from Sam's killer and we are all worried about it and also about the psychological effect it's having on Roscoe." Turning to Yuna and Fuji, she said, "while you were away, I asked Gus and Amanda to keep an eye out for that black car which appeared to be stalking him. Gus, could you tell us what you saw, please."

Gus stood up importantly, obviously planning to make a meal out of her 'report.' She began slowly, "Amanda and I thought we'd better develop a system. We knew that Roscoe never left the house before nine in the morning, but we weren't sure if the killer knew that. We started our surveillance at 8:30 each day. It was quite simple, really. We just took to eating breakfast in the living room where we had a good view of the front of Roscoe's house. One of us would serve breakfast while the other one just sat there and we took turns so we wouldn't get too tired. We stayed there until ten each day and again between three and five in the afternoons. We reasoned that if he were going to show up, those would be the logical times so he could catch Roscoe coming or going."

"The day after you left," Gus continued, turning to Fuji, "we saw a black car parked there between nine and ten. Amanda went out the back door, walked around the block and just ambled by from the other side of the street so she could discreetly copy down the license number. But after that, the black car didn't come back until two days before you returned. Then suddenly it was there every morning and afternoon. Again, Amanda checked the license plate and it was the same number. From all this, we conclude that he must have overheard my remark about you being gone two weeks (and here she did manage to blush at her rashness and impulsivity) and just gave up on finding you until after you returned home from your trip, which he thought would be a couple of days earlier than it was."

"Thank you, Gus and Amanda, for all your work and for finding out that valuable information," Claire replied. Gus sat down somewhat unwillingly, recognizing the note of dismissal in Claire's voice.

"What are we going to do?" Yuna wailed. "We can't let Roscoe go anywhere. It's too dangerous!"

"Well, Tia and I have a suggestion if Jimmy will agree," Claire said. Tia, of course, had negotiated this with Jimmy in private, in advance. The discussion had not been an easy one because of his seeming inability, for some reason, to understand why this totally private matter of concern only to their own family, that is, disposing of a house in Mexico that they didn't need, should suddenly be turned into what he perceived to be some kind of side show.

Armed with the arguments Claire had provided to her—the products of Claire's devious mind—Tia had explained to Jimmy that a regular winter holiday for the group in the same place every year where they could build community and some sense of continuity would be a great advantage for them. In terms of advantage to Jimmy and Tia, they could place the property in the hands of a property manager for the rest of the year and have it rented out, preferably to high end, long-term clients, those who were looking for more than a place to just bed down and who wanted to impress staff, clients, and family members. A four-bedroom home on the beach with extra sleeping capacity in the living room had to be a hot commodity!

Tia had gone on then to say that Claire would come along and share her expertise in terms of finding inexpensive, durable but aesthetically appropriate furnishings to give it the type of classy look that would be required to appeal to this type of clientele. Then, every year, when they had their two-week trip with the group, Claire and Tia could look after whatever refurbishing was necessary. Claire would use her decorating connections to find a reliable property manager and keep in touch with him to ensure that things would run smoothly and Jimmy wouldn't have to worry about a thing except cashing the rent checks and adjusting his annual income tax returns accordingly. But, of course, it was entirely up to Jimmy. They could all go there and if he still decided to sell they would at least have the satisfaction of knowing that they'd provided one winter holiday to three adults, including his sister, who'd had so few leisure opportunities in their lives and seen so little of the world.

If Claire's husband, Dan, had been present when Tia had been presenting these arguments to Jimmy, which had been so carefully rehearsed with her by Claire, he would have snickered. Once Claire got going on an idea for something she wanted, it was very hard to stop her and an uncharitable person might even call her somewhat diabolical in the way she set about with such determination to achieve her own ends. But that, of course, was where the diabolical analogy broke down. Claire would never argue this passionately for something for herself. It was always in situations where it was for the good of others she felt the need to champion.

"What idea are you hatching up now, Claire?" Gus asked with a sarcastic note in her voice but with a little note of hurt underneath.

Claire felt badly for not sharing with her aunt, but it had been too delicate a negotiation to risk her aunt's, sometimes limited, discretion. She replied simply. Since Jimmy now has access to this big house in Mexico right on the beach and since he needs to go down there anyway to check it out and decide what to do with it, Tia and I thought we could take this opportunity to bring Roscoe and Jimmy and Mavis down to have a winter holiday while the opportunity was still there.

The room was silent as those gathered absorbed this seemingly outrageous idea. But finally, Marion spoke. "What happens if one of them gets upset on the plane and it gets so bad the plane has to make an emergency landing?"

"Well, that's why we'll have to take extra support people. I was thinking of Anna and Tom. I'll be coming, of course, and it would still be good to have one more male along to support Bill and Roscoe."

"*I* could maybe come," Daisuke said.

"That would be great," Claire said, tentatively, looking at Fuji.

Fuji nodded his head, turning to his brother. "That would be wonderful, Daisuke! Yuna and I are not up to any more travelling right now and Roscoe gets along well with you."

"What about costs?" Marion asked.

"Well, there's no problem with continuing to pay the staff wages while they are out of the country. I discussed it with PDD. Tom, Anna and I will be working more hours than usual, but on the other hand we'll have the support from Jimmy and Tia and Daisuke, so I'm hoping with the above level of income we'll be generating and since we'll also be getting a bit of a busman's holiday out of it, we can pay our own plane fares. I've already discussed this with Tom and Anna and they think that's reasonable. I understand that Roscoe, Bill and Mavis each have enough AISH money left to pay for their plane fare and expenses. Are you okay to pay your own fare, Daisuke?"

Daisuke nodded his head silently in agreement.

"Then the only other costs are ground transportation and food. If any of us want to buy extras, souvenirs and such, well that's up to us."

Marion spoke up then. "I would love to go but with my heart condition that's not possible. However, I'm so grateful this opportunity is being provided for Bill. I want to throw an extra $500.00 into the kitty to help with the food costs and Bill, of course, will pay for his share out of his AISH money."

Gus, always competitive and never one to be out-done, sneaked a quick look at Amanda and saw the quiet nod. "Amanda and I will add an extra $500.00 between us to give you $1000.00. Do you think that will be enough?"

"If it's not, Jimmy and Claire and I will make up the difference," Tia said firmly, not even checking with the others to make sure this was okay. After all, this was all Claire's grand scheme. She could 'pay the piper' since she was the one 'calling the tune,' just to borrow one of Claire's own endless aphorisms.

Some excited discussion followed as to what they would do there for entertainment, how they would manage to meet Mavis' needs on the plane and do all the lifting of her in Mexico without a mechanical lift and so forth. But by ten that night, a rough plan was in place and everyone left happy. As it turned out, Claire, ever the optimist and incapable of controlling her impulses, had already booked the plane tickets that day with the proviso that she could change one or more of them within 24 hours at no cost. She now added one for Daisuke, having attained his passport number and the passport spelling of his name from him after the meeting. They were leaving the following Monday!

Chapter 18: The Eventful Trip to Mexico

Claire wiped her brow and looked around. All were there and accounted for. All safely strapped in—Mavis in the front row seat to her left with Anna sitting in the window seat on the far left. It had been quite an argument to convince the airline officials to allow them to sit there. The official position was that passengers seated there had to be able bodied in case of an emergency, although it was not an official emergency row with an exit. Claire had argued strongly that if Mavis should have a grand mal seizure, her head would jerk forward violently and if the person in front had his seat reclined (men being the usual recliners) she could receive a serious head injury. She won. She was used to winning.

Claire looked back at her remaining entourage seated in rows 2 and 3 on the other side of the aisle. Bill was seated in the aisle seat of row 2, with Tom, a male assistant, in the middle, and Roscoe in the window seat so he could pursue his newly cultivated hobby of photography. Directly behind Bill, Jimmy was seated, and Roscoe's uncle had the window seat behind Roscoe. In the middle sat a rather heavy man (300 pounds, Jimmy guessed) about 40 years of age. He complained loudly to the stewardess about being seated in "the handicap section" and Tia, seated directly behind Jimmy, courteously offered him her seat, even though they had all paid extra in advance to choose their seats. This elicited a headshake and a fierce scowl from Claire who'd carefully planned the seating arrangement in order to facilitate quick access to the three vulnerable individuals in the event of an incident, and the man, who had stood up hopefully, quickly sat down again.

Claire mentally vowed to give Tia a private lecture on the importance of not giving into this kind of prejudice and sense of entitlement. Tia's pre-assigned role, and the whole reason for her to be sitting in the aisle seat, was to quickly grab the emergency bag from the overhead storage unit and dispense the needed items. It held the Ativan for Mavis in case of a severe seizure, Bill's puffer in case he had an asthma attack, and Roscoe's special comfort toy, a well- worn, brown and (off)white teddy bear he called Mickey. Claire had determined that this arrangement would be the best way to avoid confusion and delay in an emergency. Mavis was unlikely to need her pills but if they were stashed in the seat back for convenience and then accidentally left behind on the plane it would be a major problem. If Bill had ready access to his inhaler, he was likely to play nervously with it and use up the stored dosage. Roscoe would be simply reinforcing existing stereotypes if he was seen to be cuddling a child's teddy bear, so this item was to be brought forth only under extreme circumstances.

It was now 10 a.m., and Claire reviewed the exhausting events of the morning. Mavis had been up since six, two hours before her usual time. She had breakfasted in her pajamas, and had then had a quick bath, shampoo, tooth brushing and dressing. Then she had been left alone on the commode for twenty minutes and had miraculously 'produced,' much to Claire's satisfaction, who had taken the necessary dietary measures to ensure this outcome the day before. In the private handicap washroom at the airport, Claire and Anna had placed Mavis on her wheelchair commode and again had been able to leave her alone for some minutes in a quiet, calm environment. As a result, she had voided fully and then been heavily diapered to cover the period of the five-hour flight and deplaning. Plane washrooms, even the so-called 'handicap' ones, were absolutely impossible for somebody like Mavis.

Bill, always anxious about any change to his routine, had been unsettled for the past three days, and the only way to keep him calm now was to allow him unfettered access to his Gameboy, something Claire usually avoided in order to interest him in other activities. Roscoe, normally the easiest of the three to reason with, had been the most difficult on this occasion. He had been irrationally fearful and untrusting, demanding to remain at home with his parents.

Claire realized grimly that after what Roscoe had gone through in the past couple of months, it would take a long time to get past what was effectively post-traumatic stress disorder. Many who knew him believed that because of his limited capacity to understand, Roscoe could not have been affected by what he had witnessed as badly as someone else with normal comprehension would have been. However, Claire argued that it was precisely this limited processing ability which made the situation so much worse and the ability to help him with it through counseling so much more limited.

The takeoff was smooth and elicited surprisingly little reaction from the three as they had been well schooled in advance as to what to expect. Claire had rehearsed it with them with a toy plane and appropriate sound-cffccts. She'd shown them pictures of the earth getting further and further away and had explained that planes were designed in such a way so the air actually supported them. She had a feeling Roscoe understood more or less what she'd said and Bill seemed to be mollified by her assurances. Mavis just enjoyed the soothing sound of her voice, the pictures and the same story being told over and over again.

Once they reached cruising altitude, Claire breathed a big sigh of relief. She settled back in her seat and rewarded herself for all her Herculean efforts of the morning and the elaborate planning which had preceded it by immersing herself in the current, cozy mystery on her iPad, *Death of a Beauty Queen,* by Barbara Jean Coast.

The sky was blue and the plane, a Boeing 737, was filled with the happy chatter of 150 cold Canadians anticipating their warm, beach holiday. Claire was just drifting off to sleep, a luxury that had been in short supply for the past three days or so, when the pilot's voice interrupted, warning of turbulence ahead. Claire turned to the others and held up both her thumbs to launch the pre-arranged plan.

Tia quickly exited despite the stewardess's warning since the seat belt sign had come on, and grabbed the emergency bag. Tom clasped hands with both Bill and Roscoe and Jimmy reached his arms around Bill through the space between the seats and clasped him firmly. Daisuke reached his arms around the top part of Roscoe's seat in front of him and began to gently massage Roscoe's neck and shoulders. Claire and Anna placed their hands on Mavis' shoulders and knees to support her and keep her from sliding forward in the seat. Claire talked to Mavis using truncated speech. "Bumps! Bumps ahead. You like bumps. Fun. Whee!"

The bumps *were* fun at first, and nothing that seasoned air travelers had not previously experienced. Claire looked around and saw that Roscoe and Bill did not seem overly concerned. Mavis was giggling joyfully. But then suddenly everything changed. The plane seemed to buck like a powerful horse, suddenly soaring upwards through the air and then dropping rapidly. It fishtailed from side to side with the tail whipping violently back and forth and the wings flapping up and down crazily. For those seated where they could see them, it appeared like they were going to break off. There was a collective gasp throughout the plane and all background chatter stopped. The plane then went through a whole series of violent up and down thrusts and lurched erratically from side to side, tipping first one way and then the other. It seemed to be engaged in a violent conflict with a malevolent force determined to hurl it to the ground and it was clearly losing altitude.

There were screams coming now from the back of the plane where the tail was fiercely lashing back and forth. An unfortunate steward, delivering a tray full of celebratory glasses of champagne, was catapulted into a row of seats, his head connecting solidly with a metal edge. His arms reflexively shot up, propelling twenty full glasses of champagne onto the ceiling, and he crumpled to the floor with his head bleeding heavily.

A stewardess at the front of the plane slammed into the doorway, severely bruising her arm and wrenching her shoulder. An overweight passenger who kept his seatbelt undone for comfort was thrust upward, his head hitting the ceiling. Through all this, the cockpit remained ominously silent as the pilot and co-pilot focused all their energies on stabilizing the plane. The rocking and rolling continued for what seemed like a long time but was really only a couple of minutes. The undamaged crew members offered no explanation or comforting words as they were busy looking after their injured partners.

Finally, the turbulence eased up but the plane still seemed to be descending. The pilot's voice came on then, explaining that they had been directed to land at a nearby regional airport so that the injured people could be medically evaluated and the plane checked over. It had taken a severe beating and damage to the wings and fuselage was likely. There were pockets of nervous chatter throughout the plane with a half dozen passengers requesting that they be allowed to leave the plane when it landed and return to Edmonton. A young girl about twelve insisted on using the washroom even though they were descending and the seat belt sign was on. Her father stood behind her arguing that it was urgent and this was the way she responded to stress. But many people in the plane remained silent, trying to process what had just happened.

Once Claire recovered her own equanimity, she checked first on Mavis. She and Anna had been supporting her with all their strength throughout the violent hurling and jumping that the plane had experienced and the pilot's sometimes equally violent efforts to stabilize it. Mavis was crying now and Claire and Anna were fully occupied trying to comfort her. Bill was struggling to get out of his chair as he always needed to pace around when he was anxious. He was rocking vigorously back and forth, much to the annoyance of the person seated in front of him, and was chanting over and over again, "Bad plane, bad plane." His game boy had been hurled down the aisle when the plane first hit the air pocket. A passenger far back in the plane held it up and a stewardess returned it to him. This soothed Bill somewhat and he began compulsively playing it, although he continued chanting to himself in a loud voice.

Meanwhile, Roscoe was ominously silent, a shocked look on his face. Then he started shaking violently. Tom raised the armrest between them and slipped his arm around Roscoe's back, despite the protests of the stewardess. Tia reached over and handed Roscoe his bear, and he wrapped both his arms around it. Daisuke rubbed and patted Roscoe's back from behind, talking to him in Japanese in what appeared to be a chant. But Roscoe was hyperventilating at this point, huffing and puffing rapidly but still panicking as if he were short of breath.

Tia grabbed the sickness bag from her seat back, stood up and held it firmly over Roscoe's mouth and nose. By this point, the plane was over the runway. It landed with a sickening bump, blowing a tire, and Tia's head hit the ceiling. The pilot immediately threw on the brakes and the force propelled Tia back into her chair, which was just as well. On a positive note, the sudden shock jarred Roscoe out of his hyperventilating trance and he sat there numbly but safe for the moment.

This new shock was too much for Bill though, precipitating an asthma attack. His breathing was coming in odd, strangled gasps and Tia handed the inhaler to Jimmy. "Breathe out!" Jimmy ordered, and demonstrated accordingly. "Out!" he said sternly, when Bill did not respond. Finally, Bill complied. "Now, in! Big breath!" he commanded, again demonstrating, and thrusting the puffer into Bill's mouth after setting up the new dose. Gradually, Bill's breathing calmed and he settled back in his chair.

The plane had continued taxiing with unusual velocity even though the pilot had hit the brakes almost immediately when they landed, pulling them on so violently that they screeched loudly. The small town runway on which they were landing had never been designed for big, international jets and basically it was too short. Finally, thc planc lurchcd awkwardly and lopsidedly to a halt. One might have expected this feat to be accompanied by relieved clapping on the part of the passengers, but the plane was oddly silent except for

Roscoe's fearful dialogue with his teddy bear. "Mickey *okay*? Mickey *okay*?"

Chapter 19: Anticlimax

There was one thought in everyone's mind as the plane finally jerked to a halt and the pilot cut the engines. They wanted off! But it was not to be. One of the crew explained over the intercom that because they had made an unscheduled stop in the United States, they would have to wait until the customs officer arrived to take them through the usual customs check. Angry groans were heard throughout the plane and the young girl with the nervous stomach threw up. The acrid smell of vomit did not help anyone's mood and the pilot turned the engines back on, ostensibly to taxi closer to the terminal, but the secondary effect was to allow the air vents to run.

Finally, more than an hour later, the custom's officer arrived, having travelled down from Billings, Montana, an hour away. He proceeded with his methodical customs check of the passengers, beginning with Claire, Anna and Mavis since they were seated in the front. He asked them if they had anything to declare. When they hesitated, he demanded to see their flight bags and triumphantly pulled out a plum, plus an apple, a banana and a baggie of sliced raw carrots and cucumber slices.

When he started to open Mavis' plastic containers of pre-ground lunch, Claire stopped him, citing contamination concerns, and he grudgingly looked at them through the sides and gave them a pass. But then, he pulled out a plastic garbage bag and asked her to toss in the banned items. "You cannot bring raw plant material into the United States," he argued. All the fruit and vegetables have to go."

"We're all going to eat our lunches now," Claire argued. "The food for the young men over there was specially prepared because of their particular dietary needs and cannot easily be replaced—and besides, they are hungry now." Mavis cried obligingly and Bill chanted "lunchtime, lunchtime." "Why don't you check the rest of the passengers and recheck us at the end?" she offered desperately. "By the time you return, I'm sure there won't be much of a problem—if any."

The customs officer suddenly became aware that the people around Claire and her group had become surprisingly quiet and he saw many hostile glances directed towards him. He realized that this was not a battle he was going to win and conceded the point. He glanced back and saw somebody in Aisle 5 holding up an apple to his mouth and gesturing to those further back, who were busily getting out their respective stashes and digging in. Meanwhile, Claire and Tia were dispensing the prepared lunches and instructing everyone to eat their fruit and raw vegetables first! She and Anna quickly ate theirs and then she called back to the customs officer who had now only progressed a quarter of the way through the plane. He came back to her grudgingly.

"We need to take Mavis off the plane. She's becoming too stressed and is likely to have a major seizure. She needs washroom facilities and access to her wheelchair and tray and a quiet place where she can eat her lunch." Claire said this is an unnecessarily loud voice to make sure the cheering squad in the first few rows heard.

"I can't allow that," he replied. "Sorry, but everyone has to leave together."

"This is likely to escalate into an urgent situation very shortly," Claire replied. I'm sure you can make an exception in this case."

"Maybe you should have thought about that before you brought somebody in her condition on a plane in the first place."

"Oh, really? And what if somebody was having a heart attack right now? Would you tell them the same thing? Rules are rules! And by the way, can you give me the website where I can look up that rule and tell me which section of the custom regulations I'd find it in? I see I have internet access."

The customs officer began to sputter out a response but it was drowned out by the various comments being volunteered by the passengers behind him. Meanwhile, Mavis was doing her part by emitting a prolonged wail. Finally, he said, "Well, it's not just up to me. The captain may have something to say about rooting around in the luggage department to find the wheelchair."

Claire turned her attention to one of the flight attendants who'd been hovering nearby. "Would that be a big problem?" she asked.

"Not at all," she replied crisply, but with a note of sympathy in her voice. "Wheelchairs are always packed last and right at the front so the ground crew can get them off quickly and ready them for unloading passengers with disabilities." She looked at the customs officer to make sure he was not objecting and then added, "I'll contact the ground crew to get the chair ready and then ask one of the officers inside to come out and escort you to the designated area." She turned to the customs officer, "How long before you're through with their customs check?"

"I need to recheck their carry-on bags for items not allowed. A couple of minutes," he replied gruffly. But

Claire had made sure to take care of all of that and he found nothing.

Within ten minutes, Claire, Anna and Mavis were being escorted off the plane. Claire gave Tia a meaningful look as she departed and Tia nodded her head slightly. When he saw Mavis leaving, Bill struggled fiercely to get out of his chair and called out, "Mae-Mae not go. I go, too!" Roscoe joined in to add to the cacophony and Claire smirked to herself. She was fairly sure that the rest of her group would be joining them in a few minutes if the assertiveness lessons she had been giving to Tia had had any impact.

A burly ground crew attendant carried Mavis gently down the steps while another one stood at the bottom bracing her chair. One of the local airline workers led them inside into the designated area set aside for the plane passengers and soon they were in a quiet room with a completely empty washroom nearby. Claire and Anna both crowed gleefully when they saw this, wheeled Mavis in and proceeded with their usual washroom routine with her in glorious privacy.

Then they fed her the prepared lunch, noting with satisfaction that the officious customs officer had overlooked the fact that Mavis' 'sandwich' contained a finely ground mixture of romaine lettuce, green onion and red pepper in addition to the ham, cheese and Dijon mustard. A smaller dish contained a ground up stick of celery and cucumber seasoned with mayonnaise and thickened with a half spoon of powdered psyllium. For dessert, Mavis had one of her staples: a kiwi ground up with half a banana. All of this would have gone in the garbage if the customs officer had realized what it was!

Mavis had just finished her meal and was leaning back resting in her tilt-in-space wheelchair when the rest of their group trouped in. Bill had continued to be very agitated after Mavis left and Roscoe was barely holding it together. It had been taking the focused effort of the four remaining support persons to keep the situation under control and at Tia's insistence, the customs officer had finally allowed them to leave.

Once they arrived, Claire took over with Roscoe. Although she had not been allowed outside the restricted area to get any additional food or water earlier, a kindly attendant had offered to go out to the neighboring cafe and bring them back anything they needed. Claire had asked for a bottle of diet Pepsi and a piece of pie for Roscoe, listing the acceptable choices in order of his preference. The attendant had returned with his favorite, coconut cream! Thus it was easy to lead Roscoe to a quiet corner and get him to sit down and enjoy his dessert before starting in on the remainder of his lunch, the non fruit and vegetable part!

Claire sat across from him with a cup of coffee and remained silent, allowing him to enjoy his meal in peace. Once he was through, she started talking to him gently about the plane drama. Her strategy was to tell him how she had felt, hoping this would prompt him to open up about his own reaction. "Wow! I was really scared when the plane started jerking around like that!" she told Roscoe. "I wondered if it would fall down even though I know how strong planes are. How did *you* feel, Roscoe?"

"I scared. I really scared. I think maybe I die—like Sam. *Poor* Sam!" Roscoe wailed. He started rocking and moaning then and Claire was very glad that the rest of the passengers had not yet been released.

"But it wasn't the same as Sam, was it, Roscoe? Nobody was trying to kill us. It was just an accident. A very rare kind of accident—that could never happen again in a million years!" Claire thought a little hyperbole was justified under the circumstances.

"Why? Why bad things keep happing to me?"

"I don't know, Roscoe," Claire said simply. "Sometimes life just is that way. But the pilot worked very hard to keep us safe. Did you see how he was sweating when he came out to talk to us! There are lots of good people in the world like him and only a few bad ones!"

Roscoe said nothing but seemed to find this satisfying. But then, after a moment, he commented, "Okay this time, but I not ride planes anymaw. Naw safe!"

This was just what Claire had been afraid of and she imagined dragging him kicking and screaming onto the new plane that was coming, and him making such a scene that the flight attendant made them get off! But she decided it was better not to discuss it with him any more right now. They still had several hours to wait until the replacement plane arrived.

"Well, that was a pretty terrible experience—but there is *one* thing," she said carefully. "You certainly don't have to worry about any black cars following us. He never would have made it through *that* storm!"

For the first time in a long time, Roscoe grinned. "Black cahs can't fly, Claih. *You* know that!"

"Well, we're going to be in Mexico for two whole weeks and he can't find us there. Don't you think it will be nice to just relax in the sun and not worry about him or Lan or anybody?"

"Y-e-sh," Roscoe said cautiously. "I'm thinking."

"Well, you carry on and think. There is lots of time until the new plane comes. And if you get bored, you can get your iPad out of your backpack and play some games or open your spelling program and study your spelling."

"Maybe I play a game," Roscoe said, with a naughty twinkle in his eyes that spoke volumes about what he thought about Claire and her academic improvement program.

"Okay," Claire said. "We *are* on holiday, after all. You carry on. I'm going over there to that quiet corner and read my book on *my* iPad for awhile." *One thing* Claire thought as she walked away. *Being in a restricted area like this I don't have to worry about keeping an eye on him. There's no other place he can go.*

Chapter 20: Mexico at Last!

The next few hours passed quickly enough.

Anna did her best to carry out Mavis' range of motion program by using the reclining function on her tilt-in-space wheelchair. It wasn't perfect for this purpose but certainly better than any alternative other than the real exercise table they had at home that adjusted up and down to accommodate the height of the care provider of the day.

After the fright on the airplane and the long day they'd already had, Bill compensated by stretching out on one of the linked banks of chairs and fell into a deep sleep. Tia wedged an airplane pillow under his head and covered him with one of Mavis' blankets they'd brought along in case she had a bad seizure and needed to sleep. The other passengers observed all this and some looked annoyed, perhaps thinking he had no right to take up four chairs even though there was plenty of extra seating. But others looked compassionate and understanding, perhaps wondering how terrible the experience must have been for him with his limited ability to understand what was happening or how he could possibly survive.

Eventually, the plane arrived and everyone trouped out of the restricted area and then back through the checkpoint which meant pulling out passports and pulling off shoes and opening up computers and dumping their water bottles. *The good thing about it,* Claire thought, *was that it created so much busywork Roscoe did not have too much time to think about what lay ahead and he climbed onto the plane meekly enough.*

"Another two hours and we'll be in Mexico!" Claire told him brightly and with only a small exaggeration. "Then we can all relax and think about what we're going to do tomorrow." Roscoe just looked at her and she had the uncomfortable feeling that he knew it was not as easy and simple as she made it sound.

The plane trip was smooth for the most part, but when it did hit a little turbulence there were gasps from various passengers. Obviously, the trauma had not been restricted to Roscoe and Bill. Claire wondered how she and the others had been insulated. Daisuke seemed to be fine, for example. But then she thought—it was because they had all been single-mindedly focused on helping the more vulnerable members of their group through it that they'd had no time to dwell on what might happen to them. *And they had done it*, she thought. *Hadn't her plan been brilliant!* She'd have to crow about it later to Tia when they were alone for a few minutes.

By the time the plane glided down over the Gulf of Mexico and the lights of Cancun came into focus, it was dark. Plane protocol required that, while Mavis had been the first to get on, she was the last to get off because of the special arrangements and time involved to move her. Jimmy and Tom stayed behind to do the lifting. Tom carried Mavis down the stairs with Jimmy a step or two in front just in case he slipped. The wheelchair was set up at the bottom and Jimmy braced it while Tom slid her deftly in. He'd had lots of practice by this time when the ceiling lift at home broke down or had been left unplugged!

The van they'd hired was waiting for them, having made the trip twice because of the accident, but it was really only a bus and more lifting was involved, as well as taking the wheels off the wheelchair for transport. Fortunately, one can do that easily with Quickie wheelchairs. Finally, an hour later, they were inching painfully over the huge traffic bumps leading into Playa del Carmen and a few minutes later were at the house.

Chapter 21: Ill-Gotten Gains?

"Oh, my God!" Jimmy said involuntarily. "What are we going to do? There's no way Megan's parents left her enough money to pay for this house!"

"We'll rent it out for most of the year and that will pay for the expenses," Tia replied.

"But..."

"Can we discuss it later in private, please? We're not even in the door yet and who knows what surprises might await us." Tia looked furtively to the side to see if Anna and Tom were paying attention and Claire saw her shoulders drop with relief when she noticed they were still busy getting Mavis settled in her chair. From the pictures Tia and Jimmy had received, they knew that there was an on-grade patio door that they could get the wheelchair through.

Jimmy looked at Tia quizzically but did not say anything further. But Claire saw the confusion and repugnance in his face and that said it all. Tia and Jimmy had known this was a substantial property and they also knew it had been paid for outright and that inherited money could not have covered the whole cost. If it were in Canada, it probably would have been confiscated once the drug connection had been uncovered, but it was in Mexico, and there was the question of the parental money so Jimmy's title to it was not being contested.

He'd seemed okay with that, justifying this lucky windfall as payback for all his suffering and also by the fact that there was no way to return it to the people who had purchased the drugs in the first place or to compensate whoever might have suffered along the way as it was harvested, prepared and transported. But faced with the reality of this elegant home, far superior to his own rather modest, establishment in Edmonton, his moral sensibilities were affronted.

Tia, on the other hand, was more pragmatic. She knew what it was to have less than what was needed. She knew what it was like to be *regarded* as less just because she was an immigrant. And for these reasons, she felt no fealty to the Canadian government. Tia and *Jimmy would have to work this clash in values out*, Claire thought. And this could be the first major test of their relationship.

Mavis and all their belongings were out of the van, the driver had been paid and had driven away and everyone was now clustered around Jimmy as he looked down at the key in his hand. Mavis was whining with fatigue and Bill looked ominously nervous and on edge. Roscoe just stood there with a dazed look on his face, too tired to even feel afraid at the moment.

Jimmy put the key in the lock. The others waited while he went inside and directly to the patio door so Mavis could enter. Tom and Anna guided her through the patio door and the rest trouped through the front door after Tia. The two groups met and clustered together in the living area in silent awe, taking in the beautifully-crafted Mexican tile flooring throughout, the white, decoratively plastered walls, the high, gracefully arched ceiling and the lustrous wooden cathedral windows. Tia noted with satisfaction that they were screened on the inside and that they opened outwards with sturdy, expensive-looking brass fittings.

Slowly, the whole group walked together through all the rooms on the main floor, oohing and aahing as they went. Tia said nothing about this but silently told herself that tomorrow she would get up early and mop the floors and make sure they were all wearing house shoes from now on. Who knew what they were tracking in. She only hoped that the appropriate cleaning supplies were in the house as she had requested in her negotiations with the property manager.

Any further admiration and examination would have to come later as there was an urgent need to get Mavis, Roscoe and Bill settled in for the night. Because Tia had received the house plan in advance, she and Claire had worked out a tentative plan and now, after a quick examination of the available bedrooms and bathrooms, they put it into action. There was a double bed and a twin bed in the master bedroom with en suite and Claire and Tia noted with satisfaction that the latter had been made up with an extra mattress to raise its height, as requested. This was where Mavis would sleep and it would also function as a change table. Whether or not it was firm enough to use as an exercise table as well was another question, but they would worry about that tomorrow.

Claire and Anna would have to share the double bed and each fervently hoped that the other was a calm and quiet sleeper. The second bedroom had a queen-sized bed and Roscoe and Daisuke would sleep there. The third one was slightly smaller and had two twin beds. Tom and Bill would share that one. At the other end of the house and down a half level was a fourth bedroom of modest size with a double bed and its own small bathroom. Jimmy and Tia would sleep there. It was now 10:30 in Edmonton but 11:30 in Mexico. Within a half hour, Mavis, Bill and Roscoe were in bed, although Bill could not brush his teeth because somehow his toothbrush had gone missing. The rest of them followed shortly.

Chapter 22: The Leisure Life

Exhausted as she'd been, Tia was up early the next morning exploring her new domain. Their room faced the pool and had a tiny balcony leading off it. She had quietly made herself a cup of coffee with the Keurig machine she'd ordered to be installed and she sat now in a chair on the balcony admiring the beautiful pool stretched out a few feet below. "No, we are not giving this away and we are not selling it. We are *keeping* it and we will use it to make a difference in people's lives, people who could not hope to know anything like this otherwise." Tia had spoken quietly but aloud to herself and she had not heard Jimmy padding up quietly behind her.

"I hear you," he said quietly. "I thought about it. There's no way we can undo what Megan did and no one to compensate for any ill the users of those drugs may have suffered as a result. All we can really do is try to bring some good out of it."

Tia kissed him quietly on the forehead. Then she left to make him a cup of coffee and when she returned they sat together on their little balcony, just breathing the air, admiring the blue sky and the pool and imagining all that this new life could bring to them and those they cared about.

Twenty minutes later, they heard a knock at the door and Claire came in carrying a carafe of coffee, a cup for herself and a plate of buttered toast with small dishes of plum jam and peanut butter on the side. "I came to discuss our plans for the day," she said, a bit defensively. She did not want to intrude on their time together but plans had to be made—and also, she really wanted to share a little of this glorious picture with them.

"What's happening with the others?" Tia asked.

"Anna and Tom are working together to get Mavis and Bill ready and Daisuke is taking care of Roscoe. Those two are already eating breakfast and the others will join them shortly. They told me I wasn't needed and the three of us should just relax and do the planning piece."

"Great!" Jimmy said. "I wasn't looking forward to being part of the maddening crowd just yet!" Tia looked at him reproachfully but Claire nodded her head in understanding. She knew full well what it meant to be a 24/7 care provider because of her daughter and she knew it took some getting used to.

"Well, what do you suggest we do today, Claire?"

"I think we need to spend the day getting oriented: examining the house and property, figuring out what other supplies we need and purchasing them and maybe just walking around town to see what the place has to offer."

"Sounds good to me. What about the others?"

"Well, there are too many of us to troop around together. We will look like a regular sideshow. I think we can leave Tom and Anna here with Bill and Mavis, and Roscoe and Daisuke can go off on their own. We three will do some exploring around here and figure out what supplies we need. Then maybe you and I and Jimmy can do the shopping, Tia. Then we'll come back here and have lunch, pick up Roscoe and Daisuke and do some exploring in the town. Tom and Anna can just have a quiet day with Bill and Mavis.

We're just a block away from the Vici Viva Resort and they have nightly shows put together by their entertainment staff. Outsiders can see them for a small fee and maybe that's something that Tom and Anna and Bill and Roscoe might enjoy this evening. They don't start until ten so I think it will be too late for Mavis, but once she rests up a bit maybe we can take her one night just to try."

"Well, that sounds like a good plan for the first day, given that we're all still pretty tired. What about tomorrow?"

"That's going to depend on Mavis and Bill and Roscoe, how well they adjust, and how well this big change of everything—air, water, food agrees with them. My priority right now is to make sure they're stable. But remember, this is a working holiday for me but it should be a real holiday for you two. You're welcome to go off on your own at any time. We can manage without you. And I know you have some business matters to settle. So why don't you just plan on having the day to yourselves tomorrow. We should be set up well enough by that time to function independently."

"Sounds good to me," Tia said and grabbed Jimmy's hand. He smiled and agreed with her.

Chapter 23: Disturber of the Peace

The days passed quickly and before they knew it, most of the first week was gone. The Three Musketeers, as Tia had taken to calling them, spent a lot of time in the swimming pool. Mavis had objected at first but now she enjoyed it. During the shopping spree that first day, Claire had come across inflatable plastic tires big enough to slip over a person's head. She had purchased two—one for Bill and one for Mavis. Bill could safely manage in the water on his own as long as he had his head and arms through the tire and Mavis could be supported safely in the water by one person once her head and arms had been pulled through the tire.

Roscoe enjoyed swimming and Daisuke stayed faithfully near him at all times just in case. He liked to swim himself for short periods but also spent a lot of time on a lounge chair beside the pool just reading, watching, listening to music and generally relaxing. Daisuke had never been any place like this before and he was really enjoying it.

On the fourth morning after their arrival, the whole group got up early and launched into frenzied preparations for an 8:30 bus trip to Xcaret, a self-described "eco-archeological theme park" located just fifteen minutes away from Playa del Carmen. Xcaret is one of the biggest tourist attractions in Mexico and was built to showcase the natural beauties of the region and the Mayan culture, traditions and architecture. It also accommodates all the bird and animal life local to Mexico including some free roaming black jaguars, safely cut off from park visitors by an impassable waterway. An artificial reef tucked behind a massive wall of heavy glass is home to most of the creatures of the sea local to the area. There are also underground rivers to swim in, snorkeling amidst the near-by reefs and, for the more adventurous, swimming with small nurse sharks or hitching a ride on a dolphin. In the evening, there is a magnificent extravaganza of a show with skilled performers representing the cultural heritage of all the different parts of Mexico.

Tia and Jimmy helped the others all they could with getting ready, but Tia had decided that they would not go along. As she had explained to Claire, even before they left Edmonton, "It's very expensive and when Jimmy and I go I want us to be able to focus on everything there without distractions. As long as you can manage without us we're not going." Claire could not object to Tia's decision since she knew that Tia and Jimmy badly needed time alone to just evaluate the whole residence in Mexico decision and this would be there only chance to do that.

Claire had researched Xcaret and the transport issue carefully before even leaving Edmonton, checking out the wheelchair accessibility of the bus and the handicap facilities available in the park. However, when they arrived, out of breath, at the bus pick-up site, Bill with his socks still in his hands and his shoes unlaced and Mavis crying and uncomfortable because she'd been rushed so much, it was only to discover that the bus was not wheelchair accessible. Claire was outraged, as she had made it very clear to the booking agent that Mavis was in a wheelchair.

The driver checked his passenger list and shook his head. He showed the list to Claire and said, "see, no handicap here."

"But I *told* the lady in the office there that we needed a wheelchair accessible bus," Claire said angrily, and pointed toward the resort office where she'd booked the tickets.

The driver pulled out his cell phone and called the office, speaking rapidly in Spanish. Claire heard an agitated female voice on the other end and after a couple of further comments and head nods the driver hung up and turned to Claire. "Elisa says you did not mention 'handicapped' to her."

"I *told* her that Mavis is in a wheelchair and we needed wheelchair access! I told her quite clearly!"

"Ah, but she not understand 'wheelchair.' She think you mean 'cane.' You should have said "handicap bus." She would have understood that."

"Then what is she doing serving English customers?" Claire said in disgust.

The driver looked angry and began to respond and Claire opened her mouth to counter whatever he was going to say, but Anna put a gentle hand on her arm. "Please let me handle this, Claire. I know what we can do."

Claire was so upset she was close to tears and she just nodded her head numbly.

Anna and the driver carried on an animated discussion in Spanish for several minutes with him checking back and forth on the phone with the woman in the resort office. Finally, Anna turned to Claire, smiling in triumph.

"The tour company will refund the money for Mavis and me and I will stay back here with her while the rest of you go".

"But it's not right that you should both miss out on the trip because of their mistake!"

"They *know* they made a mistake and caused us a lot of grief. The driver spoke directly to the resort manager and he's offered Mavis and me a guest pass to the resort for the day with all meals and amenities included. We will even have access to an empty unit so Mavis can rest this afternoon and I can attend to her personal needs in private. We will eat in the dining room and I already packed her food grinder and everything she'll need for the day so we're all set up. It'll be great and Mavis will love it!"

"Yes, that's all fine, but I'm sure you were looking forward to visiting Xcaret and it doesn't seem right that Mavis should miss out."

"But—just look at her! She's upset and disoriented. She'll be better off here alone with me. I'll get the recreation guys to help me get her in and out of the pool and I can use the built-in lift and commode unit in the wheelchair lift for dealing with her bathroom needs just like we were planning to do anyway. And as for me, I have already been to Xcaret several times in the past when I lived here. I'll be quite happy to stay back with Mavis and have a peaceful day. Coping with all of you at once is a bit much."

As Anna talked, Claire finally began to relax and calm down. She saw that she'd been so busy fighting the injustice of the situation that she had not seen the state Mavis was in and what the full implications of taking her on this complex outing would be. Without Mavis, they would not be constrained by her time consuming feeding and bathroom needs and her afternoon nap-time and would be free to enjoy all the park had to offer. Mavis would probably have a good day with Anna. Visiting the resort and meeting some new people would be a good experience and with Anna's fluent Spanish everything would be much easier. It also did not hurt that Anna was an attractive young girl and Claire had already noted that the young men working in the resort were anxious to help her.

Bill was not so easy to convince, however. He did not want to go to Xcaret without his Mae-Mae, as he thought of her, and declared that he was going to stay home, too. But this was too much for Claire who'd been planning this trip for weeks, precisely to inspire the three young people. If Mavis could not participate then at least Bill and Roscoe should have a memorable day and in the end Bill grudgingly came along.

Chapter 24: Xcaret

Xcaret turned out to be a wonderful experience. They all swam through the underground river passage with Claire and Tom pulling Bill along in the tube Claire had rented for him. Daisuke and Roscoe swam ahead stopping occasionally to tread water and rest. Although Roscoe could swim, it was more of an effort for him than most because of his low muscle tone.

After the swim, they went for their pre-arranged Mexican meal at the Incan restaurant. Daisuke and Roscoe tried a number of different Mexican dishes in small quantities. Roscoe had spent many weekends with his parents during the years he'd been in an institution and was used to trying different foods. Bill, on the other hand, was very rigid where food was concerned, part of his autistic condition. However, with Claire's urging, he did try the tortilla soup and enjoyed it. He also liked the churros, a donut-like fried pasta made in front of him in a process Bill found quite fascinating.

Claire noted with a strange combination of grudging admiration and despair the modest plate of food Tom selected. Young, slender and very athletic and health conscious, he had studiously avoided most of the Mexican dishes that tended to be quite starchy. Instead he'd selected grilled fish and a variety of cooked and raw vegetables. For dessert, he had only papaya despite the wide array of cakes, pies, cookies and puddings available, along with a panoply of fruits.

Claire, on the other hand, felt compelled to try everything and was embarrassed by the sight of her over-flowing plate. She looked down sadly at her twenty extra pounds, much of it settled on her stomach, but was unable to pass up this opportunity to explore Mexican cuisine. She didn't understand how the others could be so choosy for whatever reason. Claire, always curious and a little on edge by nature, lived with the haunting fear of missing out on something and in situations like the present one, she became a victim of this preoccupation.

After lunch, Claire opted to relax in a nearby hammock for an hour. The restaurant was situated right on the beach. She pulled out her iPad that travelled with her everywhere and immersed herself in her latest mystery—Leslie Matthews Stansfield's *Mr. Tea and the Traveling Teacup,* until gradually she dozed off. She was awakened an hour later by Tom. Tom and the others had gone for a walk through the winding trails at the forest's edge, keeping an eye out for the elusive black jaguar and finally had spotted him on the other side of the wide inlet that separated them. Bill, always observant and focused on details, had spotted him first, skimming along almost invisibly through his own chunk of rocks and trees. He was fascinated and said "Jaggar! Back Jaggar!" over and over.

Tom had been distracted by a hawker who'd managed to infiltrate this far into the reserve, although it was against the rules and to set up his impromptu shop of local wares for sale. Among the items for sale was a stuffed black jaguar replica that Bill immediately latched onto. Tom bought it for him despite his guilty thought that Claire would not approve. He thought she might say it was not normal for an adult to play with a child's toy, but Bill's enjoyment was too powerful to ignore. Bill clutched the jaguar to his breast and murmured to it. "Jackie! I call you Jackie. Jackie Jaggar. Jackie Jaggar, Jackie Jaggar, Jackie Jaggar!"

Tom and Daisuke smiled, happy to see Bill so content. Roscoe didn't seem to notice, and although Daisuke had dutifully asked Roscoe if he wanted anything the hawker was offering so he would not feel left out, Roscoe had declined. Tom said to Daisuke, "Roscoe is a really nice man. He's not jealous or greedy or envious or competitive. You can just tell that he feels worthwhile and secure. Even though he spent all those years in an institution, it's clear that his parents kept a strong connection with him and that he's always felt loved and cared for."

Tom thought he would run these ideas by Claire as they shared a common interest in psychology and particularly in personality theory. Tom had started an undergraduate degree in English a few years ago but had completed only one year before running out of money and taking his present job. He'd been much influenced by his experiences with Mavis, Bill and Roscoe, and by the many talks he'd had with Claire about the current system for helping them and what was still needed. He knew he would go back to school eventually and that he would take courses to prepare him for work in the human services sector, but he just didn't know what exact program he would choose.

The rest of the day passed in a blur. After they rejoined Claire, they all went off to visit the artificial reef to observe the various sea creatures. Bill was very taken with the sharks and when he heard that it would be possible to sit in with them in a shallow pool, he wanted to go, but Roscoe was not interested. Once Claire had been assured that Bill's sometimes unpredictable behavior would not place him at risk of being bitten by the small nurse sharks, she allowed him to go into the pool with the next group of tourists going in.

Bill was entranced. He sat along the wall in the middle of the group and just stared and stared at the small sharks swimming around and by him. Claire gradually relaxed as she saw that he was content to just look. When a shark came up to him, he just held out his hand and remained silent and inert. As a result, he ended up with more shark contact than many of his less controlled neighbors and emerged from the experience radiant with the novelty of it.

Roscoe listened to all Bill had to say but did not seem regretful that he hadn't participated. Claire sensed that he was still feeling threatened by all that had happened to him in Edmonton and didn't trust the sharks. She felt sad for Roscoe because she wanted him to have a special experience as well. She guided the group over to the dolphin tank and started talking to Roscoe in soft tones about the dolphins—how they had been seen to help drowning sailors and how gentle they were.

Roscoe watched as the dolphins dived under the various human swimmers in the tank, mostly children, and lifted them swiftly in the air. Claire saw a wistful look come over Roscoe's face and asked if he'd like to swim with the dolphins. He agreed enthusiastically and Daisuke said that he would have to go in, too, then. Once they were in the tank, it quickly became clear that they were both enjoying the experience hugely and Claire suspected that Daisuke's concern for Roscoe's safety had provided him with a face-saving reason for enjoying this novel activity as well.

"Roscoe ride!" Bill commented when a dolphin swooped under him and skimmed across the pool with Roscoe high on his back. "I go ride, too?"

Claire grabbed Bill's hand and smiled at him. "I'm sorry, Bill, but you have to be able to swim well to do that. Maybe if you practice your swimming all year and we come again, you'll be able to do that next time!"

Bill seemed contented with this and waited peacefully for Roscoe to finish and come out of the pool. When Roscoe did come out, he was grinning from ear to ear and a heavy weight seemed to have lifted from his shoulders. Claire thought to herself that the therapy the dolphins had accomplished for Roscoe had been well worth the money.

After Roscoe dressed, they all visited the Mayan Village where they had a light supper and watched the Mayan girls dancing with bottles on their heads. And soon it was time to head for the huge outdoor arena to watch the evening spectacle that was as magnificent as had been promised. It was almost 11 o'clock by the time the bus returned them to the resort and they made the short walk to their house from there. Within fifteen minutes of returning, they were all sound asleep in their beds, exhausted from the intensive day they'd enjoyed.

Chapter 25: Claire Schemes Again

The next morning, everyone, even Mavis, slept in and then over a late breakfast, they shared the preceding day's adventures. Mavis and Anna listened politely while Claire recounted their activities and the four other adventurers chipped in with their own comments from time to time. Finally, Claire looked ruefully at Anna and Mavis. "I wish you could've been there. It was *such* a good day!"

"Oh, don't feel sorry for us!" Anna said, correctly interpreting Claire's expression. *Our* day was hardly anything to complain about!" She then told them how interested all the staff had been in Mavis and how they tried to figure out things to do with her that she would enjoy. "I asked them to help me get Mavis into the pool. I thought they'd object so I explained how much she enjoyed the pool at the house. But they weren't holding back because they were afraid to take her into the water. Oh, no! What they wanted to do was take her into the ocean, so two of them carried her right across the sand and into the waves and then they stayed with her for about fifteen minutes, swinging her back and forth in the water and splashing her from time to time. And Mavis loved it! See, I have pictures."

"You mean you weren't in the water with her?" Claire asked, her eyebrows raised.

"No," Anna said, somewhat defensively. "There were two of them with her at all times and sometimes three. And besides, by the look on Mavis' face, she was enjoying all that male attention and I don't think she would have wanted me there! I stayed on the beach and took pictures as they suggested."

Jimmy smiled at this and said, "You did the right thing, Anna. We can't always be smothering her. What else did you and Mavis do yesterday?"

"Well, after that, we all went to the snack pavilion and Mavis had some guacamole and some nachos soaked in hot water to soften them and then dipped in salsa. She really digs that hot sauce! And she had a beer to swallow it down with. She drank practically the whole glass without spilling any!"

Anna had again looked a bit fearful when she revealed this latter item, but Claire just reached over and patted Mavis on the arm. "Drinking beer in the middle of the day, huh, Mavis? A girl after my own heart!"

Anna smiled in relief and then went on talking. "But you haven't heard the best part yet! After the guys saw how much Mavis enjoyed the water, they suggested we take her for a Catamaran ride. They wanted to take her alone but I insisted on going along. Well, you should have seen Mavis! The water was quite choppy and sometimes the waves slopped right over us when we got going fast. But Mavis just laughed. Once I saw her licking her lips and looking quizzical. It was as if she were tasting the salt in the water. And the water was really warm. It was almost like a bathtub!"

"Oh, that's great!" Claire burbled. "But I guess you didn't get any pictures."

"Oh, but I did!" Anna said, smugly. "I left my camera with one of the guys on the beach and he took pictures as we were coming in. Some of them didn't turn out too well as there was so much spray, but one of them is quite clear." Anna grabbed her camera and quickly flicked to a picture of Mavis with a broad grin on her face as water cascaded over her head!

"Mae-Mae have fun, too!" Bill said gleefully, and he reached over and squeezed her arm. Everyone else endorsed his sentiments.

"What about the restaurant?" Claire said. "How did she do there?"

The servers were great! I left Mavis at the table while I went to get her food, and later on my own food, because it was too crowded to push her around in there and one of the serving staff kept an eye on her for me. Then, after I finished grinding her food, another server whipped the grinder away and washed it without me even asking. And when one of them noticed how much she was enjoying the guacamole and later the papaya, they brought her second helpings. Mavis also tried some white wine and she enjoyed that as well. After lunch, we went back to the very nice room they assigned to us so Mavis could attend to her bathroom needs and have a rest. I just called in one of the cleaning staff working in the hall and he came in and helped me lift her onto the bed. After that, we went for a long walk and then visited the gift shop." Anna showed them the pretty top she'd purchased for Mavis and they all *oohed* and *ahed* appreciatively.

"And by that time, it was happy hour, I suppose," Claire said dryly. Anna nodded her head and everybody laughed.

"We did go to the main bar then because that's where all the action was. Mavis had a virgin Pina Colada and she really liked it! And several people came over to meet her. One lady came and talked to me and said she had a daughter like Mavis at home, but she'd never thought of bringing her to a resort. Some of the guys wanted me to bring Mavis to the show in the evening, but she was pretty tired by that point so we came back to the house after supper and just hung out until you all got back."

By the time they'd all finished talking and sharing, it was 11 o'clock and Daisuke and Roscoe left for a pre-arranged archery lesson. Mavis and Bill headed for the pool with Anna and Tom. Tia and Jimmy decided to walk into Playa del Carmen and invited Claire to join them, but she declined, stating that she was too tired after yesterday's adventures.

Chapter 26: The Chichen Itza Adventure—Or Not

Once everyone had left, Claire suddenly recovered and walked determinedly towards the resort. After everyone but her had reassembled for lunch at 1:30 and were wondering where she was, Claire returned, sporting a t-shirt with Vici Viva on it and a silver necklace. She was carrying a Mexican blanket folded over her arm and had a fancy sombrero on her head. There was a large grin on her face, half guilty and half triumphant.

"What did you *do*?" Tia asked. She knew that look.

"Dan and Jessie and I are now members of Vici Viva Resort! Next time you come here, we can all come along and we'll have our own place—and we can even invite you over for dinner one night, they said."

"Oh, I'm sure they'd be happy to give us a free meal if that's what it takes to suck you in!" Tia said sarcastically. "Does Dan know?"

"Well, I thought I'd wait until I got home to tell him. It's hard to explain all the details over the phone."

"Uh, huh!" Tia said, and Jimmy chortled.

"And what other loot did you get for whatever big bucks you have committed to?"

Claire blanched a bit at that, recalling the exact sum, but then went on cheerfully. "I got two free tickets for bus transportation and a guided tour of Chichen Itza and a Mexican lunch included. I was hoping you could go with me, Tia," Claire said, looking at Tia meaningfully.

"It depends. When is it?"

"Tomorrow."

"Tomorrow! What if I have other plans?"

"Do you?" Claire asked anxiously.

After a pregnant pause, Tia responded, "No. But I could have. You really don't believe in consulting anybody about your plans in advance, do you? I wonder what Dan's going to say? And why did you pick tomorrow?"

"It's a Mexican festival day and they're having a special parade in Mérrida, which is where the lunch is. I thought we might be there in time to take part in it," Claire said, but the look she gave Tia telegraphed that there was more and Tia should keep quiet.

After lunch, Jimmy uncharacteristically went down for a nap. Maybe he expected Tia to follow and maybe he really was tired, tired as in finally being away from his daily grind long enough to let down enough to actually *feel* how tired he'd become. Tia chose to believe the latter and went along with Claire for a walk when she asked. Obviously, there was a serious conversation they needed to have.

"Why tomorrow—and why Chichen Itza?" Tia hissed as soon as they were out of earshot.

"Oh, we are not going to Chichen Itza. We are getting off at Mérrida when the bus stops there for lunch."

"And how are we going to explain that to the rest of them, particularly Jimmy?"

"We're not. I bought a guidebook about Chichen Itza.We can study it on the bus and be able to tell them all about it when we get back."

You know, Claire, you judged me for lifting a tea bag or bun or a few cold cuts at a hotel complimentary breakfast in order to have something later for lunch, but don't you think your constant lying is even worse? It has gotten positively pathological in the last couple of years! Why can't we just tell them what we need to do and then buy our own tickets and go to Mérrida some other day? The bus fare there isn't that expensive. The big expense is the entrance fee to Chichen Itza—which I, frankly, would like to see."

"Oh, you innocent! You've obviously forgotten what it's like to be married—or else you don't know what it's like yet to be married to somebody who actually cares, your ex-husband being the self-centered, overgrown boy that he was! Men become protective, which is another word for saying they become controlling. They justify this behavior by saying they have your best interests at heart—which is another way of saying that they don't really see you as an adult capable of taking care of yourself. Then you have only three choices. You can either live inside the cocoon they create for you and go through life feeling semi-depressed—or you can divorce them—or you can get sneaky. If you love them, you soon realize that they're not going to change because they can't help being the way they are. The only way around the situation is to get sneaky when it really counts, like now. And surprisingly in the end, they'll often say you were right to do what you did. At least, Dan has done that on occasion.

Tia sighed because she knew Claire was right. There was no way Jimmy would agree to Tia snooping around a suspicious factory in Mérrida. "Fine," she said resignedly. "What exactly is the plan—and why tomorrow, by the way?"

"Because it's a national festival day and there will be few if any people left in the factory after lunch. So we can either ingratiate ourselves to the one or two underlings who are left, or sneak around and explore if there's nobody there—except probably a guard we'll have to avoid."

"And what if we're caught?"

"Well, we'll just have to talk our way out of it—act like dumb tourists."

"You *do* realize that there are a fair number of 'dumb tourists' already in Mexican jails—and quite a few more who are dead!"

"We'll just have to be extra careful then, won't we?" Tia looked skeptical but Claire went on, "I can't see any other option if we want to get answers so we can protect Roscoe. Can you?"

"No," Tia sighed. "But I have a bad feeling about it."

Chapter 27: A Claire Adventure Is Never Simple

The next day at 8:30, they were back at the same bus stop at the Vici Viva resort—the one for the Xcaret trip. They shared a bench seat half way down the bus and spent the trip to Mérrida assiduously studying the Chitchen Itza book instead of looking at the scenery, not that the scenery in this arid part of the Yucatan Peninsula was exactly that inspiring—mostly the scrubby remains of a dried out and much harvested jungle.

The Mérrida lunch and entertainment was very pleasant but they had a tough time enjoying it, preoccupied as they were for planning how to find and reach the processing plant without being too obvious about it and how to explain to the bus driver why they needed to stay behind in Mérrida in the first place.

When Tia left the table for a washroom break, Claire grabbed the opportunity to talk to the bus driver, seated at a nearby table in the restaurant. She explained that her friend had developed a bad case of diarrhea and did not feel comfortable going on to Chitchen Itza. They would stay behind and buy some necessary supplies for her in the town and maybe stop in an air-conditioned hotel for tea and good bathroom facilities.

The driver nodded sympathetically. This was, after all, a common tourist affliction in Mexico. He said he would watch for them on the way back and wait at the designated stop until 6:10 for them to come on board, but he would not be able to wait longer than that. When Tia returned from the washroom, she saw the driver looking at her sympathetically and she regarded Claire suspiciously.

"What did you tell the driver?" she hissed.

"Let's go outside and visit some of those kiosks," Claire responded. Once safely away from the group, Claire explained and predictably Tia exploded.

"Why me? Why do I always get to be the fall guy in your little schemes?"

"I don't do it on purpose," Claire said. "It just seems to work out better that way—to come across more plausibly, you know."

In a few minutes, Tia calmed down and said, "Well, if we're going to go, we better get going now."

"Oh," Claire said. "They have some very nice things in that Kiosk over there. We could just take a look."

"What for? We can't buy anything. Remember, we might have to make a run for it." She dragged Claire away and headed determinedly towards a gas station about a block down the road, thinking they should be able to get directions there. It gave her some small satisfaction to see the look of disappointment on Claire's face. *She should experience some small sense of loss once in awhile* Tia thought, *to make up for all the grief and embarrassment and risk her schemes often cause me.*

The man at the gas station looked at them in surprise when they asked directions to the Mérrida Sunflower Oil Factory because it was clear they were walking. "It's too far to go on foot and nobody will be there anyway because of the parade this afternoon."

But Claire was ready for this response. "We're just visiting Mexico for a couple of weeks from Canada and arranged to meet a dear friend who's working there now. She thought we better come there because we wouldn't be able to find each other in the crowds downtown today." This sounded credible to her ears but then the garage man tried to be helpful, and, as Claire told Tia later, "threw a wringer in the works."

"What's her name?" he asked. "Maybe I could call her and she could meet you here. That would be easier for you. It's a big building and even when you get there you could still have trouble finding her."

"Oh," Claire said, after a slight hesitation discernible only to Tia's ears. "I doubt if you'd know her. She's only been here a few months. She's staying with some cousins in a small town near there. I forget the name. She just wanted to feel what it would be like to be a part of Mexico. Her parents emigrated to Canada with her when she was just a baby but she grew up hearing all about Mexico and felt she needed to come here for a while to experience her heritage." After a slight pause to let this sink in since the man's English was serviceable but far from perfect, Claire went on. "If you could just call us a taxi, I think that would work best. She said she'd meet us at the main door of the factory."

The man gave them a funny look that sent an odd shiver down Tia's back, but he went inside to call the taxi and soon they were on their way. When they arrived at the factory, there was no "friend" waiting at the main door and the taxi driver offered to stay until they connected, saying that there would be no easy way to find their way back if the friend turned out not to be there. But Claire assured him it wasn't necessary and asked for his card, saying she'd use her cell phone to call him if, "by any slim chance" the friend turned out not to be there.

Once the driver left, they took a good look at the building. All the time Claire had been talking to the driver and paying him off, Tia had been scanning the windows searching for any sign of movement but she'd seen none. They approached the front door hesitantly but found it locked. Then they skirted around the building trying all the other entrances but none were open. Then Claire said in a louder than necessary voice, "Well, I guess nobody's here. We better leave. I'll call the driver and we can start hiking back down the road." She pulled out her phone and ostentatiously dialed a number but didn't push 'talk.' They walked away with Claire still holding the phone to her ear.

As soon as they rounded the first corner where they were no longer visible from the building, Claire put the phone away and motioned to Tia that they were doubling back. They approached from behind the building using as much bush cover as possible. Claire had seen a second story window open on their initial tour around the building and they approached it cautiously.

Claire said to Tia, "If I boost you up and you stand on my shoulders you should be able to crawl through. Then you should be able to creep downstairs and open a door for me."

"Why me?" Tia asked. "Why can't I boost *you* up?"

"Because I'm bigger than you."

"Well, you may be heavier but you don't necessarily have more muscle."

Claire just looked at her and Tia did as she was asked but with one parting shot. "What if an alarm goes off when I open the door?"

"Then we run like hell and hope for the best!"

But no alarm went off and together they stealthily explored the factory. Finally, they entered a big room on the second floor that was clearly a manufacturing centre and there they found the bottles. Tia exclaimed, "Look how cleverly they fit together! Some are normal bottles but on this conveyer belt you can see the two part bottles and they're transparent. They must put the coloring on afterwards!"

Claire was about to reply when they heard a downstairs door open, and hushed voices as what was clearly a couple entered. "I thought you locked this door?"

"I'm sure I did."

"Well, obviously you didn't! You better be more careful in the future. If the boss finds out you'll get fired."

The man didn't respond to that directly but said instead, "I'm going upstairs to package up some of those bottles that were left on the belts."

"What are we going to do?" Tia hissed

"We could hide in that closet. Maybe he won't look there."

"And maybe he will. I saw a women's bathroom next door. Quick, let's go!" And Tia tiptoed as quickly as she could to the door and out with Claire right behind her. They'd just entered the bathroom when they heard footsteps in the hall and Claire remembered only then that they'd forgotten to turn the lights out.

Soon they heard the man yelling for his partner who'd been the last one in that room before they left. "You left the lights on up here. I'm not the only one getting careless!" By the tone of the woman's response, it was clear that she was denying it but she came bounding up the stairs to check it out.

"The stairwell is just two doors down," said Tia, ever the observant one. If we move fast once she goes in the room we can make it."

The woman entered the room and they could hear the two of them arguing with the sounds painfully close. "Now!" Tia hissed. They ran on tiptoes down the hall and around the corner and then raced down the stairs and out the door. They didn't stop running until they reached the shelter of the surrounding forest and then stood panting fearfully. They saw the door open that they'd just left, and both the man and woman stood there for a minute looking around carefully. They breathed a sigh of relief but it was not to last.

Claire turned around because she thought she'd heard a small sound, and stared right into a gun muzzle pointed directly at her face.

Chapter 28: The Long Arm of the Law

"Police! Stand still and put your hands on your head," the man ordered. They complied, Claire still grasping the two-part bottle she'd grabbed as she left the upstairs room.

"Come with me!" he demanded, and marched them towards his car, still holding the gun on them. He opened the back door. "Get in!" They had no choice but to comply and as soon as they were inside, he pushed buttons on a remote control that locked the back doors and raised the security window between the front and back seats. Then he got in the car and drove back down the road towards Mérrida, radioing ahead for assistance.

They stopped at a large, unmarked building in town and were met by three men holding semi-automatic rifles. Their driver unlocked the doors and ordered them out, marching them towards the building. Claire was still stubbornly holding the bottle. She no longer knew why at this point. They were placed in separate interview rooms and the driver came into the room that held Claire and her bottle.

The man started a tape machine and began talking into it. "This is Inspector Delfino Romero and the female suspect in the room is being interviewed in connection with an ongoing drug surveillance operation at the Mérrida Sunflower Oil Plant. The date is Wednesday, March 27th, 2014 and the time is 3:45 p.m." Claire groaned when she heard this, realizing that there was no way now to catch the bus back to Playa del Carmen.

"What is your name and where are you from?"

"I'm Claire Burke from Canada." Claire had decided that the best strategy was to provide as little information as possible so she didn't mention Edmonton.

"What were you doing at that factory?"

Claire mentally debated the merits of sticking with her original lie, but then answered simply, "I had business there."

"What kind of business?"

"A company I'm involved with in Canada imports oil from that factory. Since I'm down here in Mexico on holiday, I thought I'd visit it out of curiosity."

The man didn't look as if he believed her, and left the room to find out what information his colleague was getting with the other suspect. Five minutes later, he returned, looking less suspicious this time. "Your friend has told us everything so you needn't bother holding back—and your 'good character' has been confirmed by our Edmonton contact."

"And that would be?"

"Inspector Donald McCoy." Claire groaned.

"He assured us that your greatest offense was being a busybody!" The policeman couldn't hold back a small smirk when he said this.

"And did he also tell you that Tia and I solved the last two cases we worked on together while he was busy charging off down the wrong trails?" Claire asked heatedly.

"No, but he *did* say that the police had had to rescue you both from a couple of close calls with the killers."

"Humph," Claire said, not deigning to argue further. "Well, would you like to know what I know about our current killer and the drug ring he's involved in or would you prefer to be like Inspector McCoy and just assume I'm some silly woman who doesn't know what she's doing? I hear Mexican men are pretty sexist!"

"Actually, I *would* like to know what you and your friend have uncovered so far. Whatever your ways, it took a lot of guts to sneak into that factory and some ingenuity to get away without being caught. I don't think they saw you when they came to the door and what's more important, I don't think they saw me. We've had them under surveillance for months, but so far we can't see anything really suspicious about their comings and goings."

"That's because they're manufacturing two different kinds of bottles that look identical from the outside," and at this point Claire held the bottle she'd been carrying over to him. "We found heroin in the bottom compartment of an identical bottle in Edmonton and it had the address of the factory here in Mérrida on it—which is why we're here." Claire then updated him on what had happened so far in their unofficial investigation including the death of the teenager Sam, the close call she and Roscoe had had, and the man in the black car who seemed to be stalking him.

Inspector Romero spoke into the tape recorder again, at this point stating that he was leaving the room briefly. When he returned, he said to Claire, "Okay, your friend's story matches yours, so we'll assume for the moment that it's substantially true. The next question is, 'What are we going to do with you?'"

"You can let me use the phone for one thing so I can contact the people we're with who'll be worried sick when we don't get off that bus when it arrives." Claire went on, speaking half to herself, "We were shopping and lost track of the time and the bus left without us."

Delfino Romero smirked. "I don't think you need to worry about that. The bus driver got really anxious when you didn't turn up and contacted the station here.

He gave us your names and contact information so we were able to let your people know what happened and that, depending on the results of the interrogation, we'd either be driving you back later this evening or incarcerating you."

Claire groaned again. "Why is it that other people can lie and get away with it but not me? *Never* me!?!" she muttered to herself, but Romero heard her and concealed an involuntary chuckle by suddenly clearing his throat.

A while later, Tia was brought into Claire's room by the man who'd been interviewing her. Inspector Romero introduced him to Claire as Sergeant Cruz Mendoza and then introduced himself to Tia. "Well, where do we go from here?" Claire asked, some of her old, take-charge attitude returning.

"*We* don't go anywhere!" Romero responded. "What *you* can do," he said, looking at Claire, "is to report any further sightings of that black car and take every precaution to protect yourself and the young man you mentioned—Roscoe. What *you* can do," and he looked at Tia, "is to stay far away from that café in Edmonton. It's far too dangerous for you to remain involved there or with those people in any capacity."

Romero went on to say, "I have informed Inspector McCoy of all your findings to date and he's quite disappointed that you did not see fit to share them with him directly."

"Why?" Tia said, acidly. "He's never been able or willing to help us in the past."

"Well, he seemed quite sincere about helping you now. He said something about political implications if anything happened to Roscoe."

"Uh-huh," Claire said, sardonically. "Let us just say that you don't know him like we do. That sounds like a typical McCoy motivation. He only acts when not acting would make him look bad."

"Well, I'm not going to get into a discussion about the character of a fellow officer with you," Romero said stiffly. Softening a bit, he added, "the bottle you grabbed from the factory is helpful to us. It's quite ingenious how they managed to form two compartments in one bottle. And I don't know about the colored ones you saw at that restaurant. You wouldn't have a picture, I suppose?"

Tia pulled out her cell phone and showed him several as well as various shots of the store layout. After examining the bottle shots closely, Romero called in an officer and sent the phone off to have the pictures downloaded onto a computer. "I can see how, looking at those colored bottles, you wouldn't be able to tell that there was anything in them but oil," he said. "But thanks to you two, we now know their secret. Too bad there's no evidence of the heroin."

"I can put you in touch with the man who analyzed it for me," Claire said.

"Yes, I'd like to talk to him, but unfortunately his findings won't stand up in court. The evidence trail has been contaminated."

Chapter 29: Facing the Music

Their police driver drove swiftly, clearly above the speed limit, and in an hour and fifteen minutes, they arrived at their door in Playa del Carmen. They started to thank him preparatory to getting out of the car, but all he said was "Wait!" He got out himself and unlocked the car doors with his hand on his gun and ordered them out. Then he marched them to the door.

"This is not necessary," Claire sputtered.

"Orders!" he said curtly. Jimmy opened the door and the policeman flashed his badge and demanded to see some id. "The names don't match!" he said.

"No. Tia and I aren't married yet, but I have here the original plane reservation list (which he'd found in Claire's room). You can see we all travelled together."

The officer studied it suspiciously and then conceded the point. "Good night," he said, and left abruptly.

"Tia, I'd like to talk to you in our room, please," Jimmy said, taking her by the elbow. He continued to ignore Claire completely. Sounds of a serious argument emanated from the room, causing Bill to pace around nervously, Mavis to cry and Roscoe to look scared. Tom and Anna and Daisuke were clearly embarrassed and Claire just felt sick, and retired to her room for the night. She was just dozing off when she heard the door open and Tia came in.

"Move over, Claire," she said tersely. "I'm sleeping here tonight."

The next day was not much better with Jimmy walking around with a face like a thundercloud and saying nothing and Tia mutely throwing herself into cleaning and organizing tasks, some of them quite unnecessary. Claire caught up on paperwork and left Anna and Tom and Daisuke to cope with 'The Three Musketeers'. But that evening, Claire pulled herself together and called a group meeting. Jimmy at first refused to attend, but finally came out and sat in a corner sulkily.

"Look!" Claire started. "What happened yesterday is what happened. Tia and I did what we thought we had to do to move the investigation along. This is not like the other investigations we've been involved in because one of our own is being directly threatened." Claire purposely did not mention Roscoe's name since he was watching TV but within earshot. She went on, "We have four days left of this very expensive holiday and I want us to make the most of it. We owe it those three," she said, pointing in the direction of the living room where Roscoe and Bill were sitting together, with Mavis in her chair beside Bill. "Now what do you suggest we do to make tomorrow special for them and what is on our must do list for the rest of the week?"

Claire's tactic worked and they did have some interesting times after that, including a daring trip to a cabaret in Playa del Carmen one evening with everyone attending but Jimmy, and a jungle tour on ATVs, during which they saw many monkeys and various bird species in the trees, had a swim in a Mexican cenate, and a visit to a Mexican family's casita. They also saw a tree snake—not the most pleasant part of their trip.

On the final day, they took a ferry trip to Cozumel and Tom and Anna went on a snorkeling tour. Roscoe tried to get used to the snorkel but couldn't master it, so Daisuke stayed behind with him and they did some shopping in the town so he could get gifts for his parents. Awkwardly, Claire and Jimmy were left to care for Bill and Mavis. They also spent the time shopping, Cozumel being somewhat of a souvenir mecca, and Claire having a substantial list of people she wanted to bring something back for. Tia had remained at the house, citing the need to get organized for the trip home the next day. It was clear that the rift between her and Jimmy was serious and Tia had confided in Claire that she was no longer sure that she wanted to go ahead with the wedding since Jimmy clearly could not accept her for who she was. She also acknowledged that Claire had been right about the limitations of men.

Chapter 30: Where Do We Go From Here?

The trip home was uneventful and Dan, Roscoe's parents and Marian and her daughter, Hilda, all turned up at the airport to transport them home. Claire threw herself into Dan's arms and for the first time since 'the incident' she started to feel warm. They had been in regular communication by phone and he knew all that had happened. He didn't like it any better than Jimmy, but he knew Claire and he'd learned to trust her and respect her instincts.

Dan knew that they'd been at an impasse in their investigation in Edmonton and the Mexican factory was the only lead they had left. True, Claire had not told him in advance because she knew that he, too, would object but when he looked at the situation from her perspective he wondered what else they could have possibly done. And besides, Claire was Claire and in the end he loved her. Claire begged Dan to speak to Jimmy when he had a chance and try to make things right. She was feeling horrible about the damage this adventure had done to his relationship with Tia.

The very next day, Claire visited Amanda and Aunt Gus to bring them their presents and find out what had been happening with the black car in their absence.

Aunt Gus was pleased with the Mexican silver picture frame that Claire had brought her and said she had a favorite picture of herself she was going to put in it. Claire smiled secretly to herself at this typical Aunt Gus response. Amanda also appeared to like her gift, a hand-made Mayan carving of a fierce-looking god for her wall. "It reminds me of the Russian ballet teacher I had when I was a child. She had the same hooked nose!" she said. Claire thought it was a rather odd comparison to make, but Amanda sometimes came out with these totally strange connections, occupying a kind of middle ground between Mrs. Malaprop and Jane Marple. Maybe that was why she and Aunt Gus seemed to make such a good pair.

"I can't stay long," Claire said. "I have to get Roscoe organized for the day. We're going back to the art workshop today. It will be his first day back in almost a month and I'm hoping he'll be okay with it. But tell me, did you see the black car when we were away?"

"He came around the first couple of days after you left, but I haven't seen him since," Amanda said.

"I'm afraid he was back this morning, just parked and idling for about ten minutes at about eight. You were in the shower, Amanda."

"He must have seen the DATS buses coming through to pick up Bill and Mavis for their day programs and figured out that we were home again," Claire speculated. "That means he must live around here somewhere." She opened her computer and quickly sent off an e-mail.

"Who are you telling?" Gus asked astutely.

"Delfino Romero. The policeman I met in Mexico." Finally, Claire had found an inspector who'd listen to her. Too bad he was 2500 miles away.

"Oh, you mean the one who arrested you?" Gus asked.

Claire raised her eyebrows.

"Jimmy told us all about it," Gus explained. "Boy, was *he* steamed! But don't worry. I calmed him down. I told him that's just the way you are, and described some of the tricks you pulled on Dan through the years so you could get information you needed. He even laughed a couple of times."

"And I told him how worried you were about Roscoe. And how hard you'd been trying to protect him," Amanda added. "I think he left feeling a little better about what you and Tia pulled off."

"Thanks, guys," Claire said soberly. "I really feel bad for Tia. I've asked Dan to speak to Jimmy, try to explain. He said he would."

"Tia should have told him and then insisted on going anyway if he objected," Aunt Gus said. "She needs to set the ground rules if that relationship is going to work. It's not the same as it is with you and Dan because Dan can always hold Jessie over your head and get you to back down if you tell him these things beforehand. Jimmy can't do that with Tia. Worse case scenario, if something happened to her, Mario's grandparents would take him in a heartbeat. Dan couldn't cope with Jessie on his own and still work and you and Dan don't have any parents to back you up like Tia does."

"We honestly didn't see it as dangerous," said Claire. "The worst we thought would happen if we were caught was embarrassment and maybe a few uncomfortable hours in a Mexican police station, which is exactly what *did* happen. We're adults and we chose to take that risk. Men take risks all the time and they don't ask permission first. How about snowmobilers in the mountains who climb up as high as they can on their big machines and sometimes end up buried in avalanches and dying. Can their wives stop them from going? No—even though everybody knows it's a stupidly dangerous sport. And they're just doing it for the thrill. We were running a bit of risk because we're trying to save Roscoe from getting killed like his friend!"

"Well, from the way Jimmy talks, I think it triggered something far deeper than just a difference of opinion. He felt abandoned and betrayed—again!" Amanda said.

Claire hung her head, remembering all Jimmy had suffered with his first wife. "I hadn't thought of it *that* way," she said.

"Well, don't worry too much. I think he's beginning to come around. Tia also talked to us and I guess she had some choice things to tell him during that big blow-out they had—about not being owned or treated like property or allowing somebody else to run her life after all these years of being on her own."

Claire left feeling better than she had since the Mérrida fiasco and with her head finally clear enough to seriously begin to consider their options from here on in for keeping Roscoe safe and finding the killer. Dan did carry through with his promise to talk to Jimmy and one way or another, the rift between Tia and Jimmy seemed to be closing and he was soon able to talk to Claire civilly.

Chapter 31: A Team Effort

The whole row with Jimmy had sobered Claire, but it hadn't lessened her resolve. And that resolve only strengthened when Amanda and Gus reported seeing the black car two more mornings that week. As Gus had mentioned, the first most recent sighting had started their second day back after almost a two-week hiatus, so that made three times altogether within an eight-day period. If, as Claire speculated, the driver lived close by they just needed to find out where before he figured out their daily routine sufficient enough to catch Roscoe off guard somewhere. But how could they find him without being too obvious about it and increasing the risk to all of them? *Hmm*, she thought. *I think we need to have a groupthink on this.* And maybe it'll have the secondary advantage of helping Jimmy to see that the Mérrida caper was more an act of desperation than an irresponsible whim.

The group met on Saturday afternoon at the home of Tia and Jimmy. Present were Roscoe's parents and his Uncle Daisuke and also Roscoe's older brother, Randy. Like many children of immigrants, Randy had changed his birth name *Ren* to the very English *Randy*. His two teenaged sons, Thomas and Gerald, were also present. *Strange,* Claire thought. *Randy had in the past made it quite clear that his sons were to be referred to by their full names, not by any of the usual abbreviations*. And somehow that made those very English sounding names fit better into the more formal Japanese culture than into the much more casual, laid-back Canadian culture.

Also present were Gus and Amanda, Marian and her daughter, Hilda, Jimmy, Tia and Tia's son, Mario. "He sometimes comes up with some good ideas," Tia had said. "And we need some good ideas right now." Claire had agreed. Dan was also there since Claire was able to arrange for Jessie's care provider to stay at their home until six and give Jessie her dinner. Claire and Tia had talked privately and strongly felt that their husbands needed to be part of the discussion in order to fully appreciate the seriousness of the situation.

Gus spoke first at Claire's invitation. Claire had reasoned that Gus really needed the limelight and Amanda didn't care much about things like that. Claire was gradually learning to understand the fragile underpinnings of Aunt Gus' personality that were hidden beneath her often irritating narcissism.

"Since we first noticed that black car stopping down the street lots of mornings, which was just a few days after a car tried to ram Claire and Roscoe, we've been keeping notes on it—which days it came and when it came and left." Gus didn't mention that it was mostly Amanda who did the watching and note-taking since she was very busy in the early morning getting stylishly dressed and fixing her hair and make-up for the day. "And Hilda here put it all into a graph for us and just look at it!" Gus produced the colored graph with a flourish and the result was a collective gasp from those present. In an instant, the connection of the black car to Roscoe went from speculative to undeniable.

Gus was obliged to sit down at this point as people were now talking openly back and forth about this ominous data. Claire was trying to call for order when suddenly Amanda stood up. She stood there quietly beside Claire and held her hand up and gradually people noticed and the room became silent.

"I would like to share something else with you but I'm not sure it means anything, so I have not even mentioned it to Gus." Claire noted the quick, reflexive scowl on Gus' face. "I don't know if he came by before your trip or not because I was not really looking for anything but the car. In the last little while, since you've been back, Claire, I have seen a young fellow on a bicycle riding by almost every day between three and four in the afternoon. He would be around your age," and Amanda waved vaguely at Randy's sons, and he is also Oriental." Claire winced at this description but recognized that Amanda was only using the language she knew, not trying to be derogatory in any way.

Gus interrupted at this point, saying dismissively, "He probably just lives in the neighborhood and goes to the local high school and passes here on his way home. Or maybe he even goes to that junior college near here. I think you're making too much of it, Amanda."

"Y-e-e-s," Amanda said slowly. "I thought so, too, and that's why I did not mention it to you. But a couple of times lately, he's come down the street the opposite way. Now why would he do that if he was just heading home from school? Wouldn't he go the same way?"

"It *is* curious," Claire commented, more to placate Amanda than for any other reason since her attention was firmly focused on the black car."

"May *I* say something?" Mario asked. Claire nodded and he went on. "I heard you tell mom that this person must live in the neighborhood since he only started coming back after you returned from the trip. But what if he just lives somewhere on the handicap bus routes and he followed one of the buses to Roscoe's house? I come home from school after three, and I've noticed that Bill's bus comes down the street from the north side and Mavis' bus comes up the street from the south side. Maybe he's trying to figure out if Roscoe is on one of those buses. Did you ever see a bus unloading when he passed by, Mrs. Roche?"

"As a matter of fact, I have, now that you mention it, Mario. I just didn't make the connection because he goes by on his bike quite quickly. He doesn't sit there like the guy in the black car."

"Thank you, Mario and Amanda. You have certainly given us something else to think about. Are there any other comments?" Claire asked.

"Uh, yes," Randy's oldest son, Gerald, said, nervously clearing his throat. He turned to Amanda. "I'm 19 and my brother, Thomas, is 16. He's still in high school, the one right near here, but I go to the junior college and it's not very far away either. You could easily bike from there to here or even further. So what I'm getting at is, how old do you think this guy was? Was he more like Thomas' age or more like my age?"

Amanda looked at Gerald carefully and then said slowly, "Well, it's hard to tell. You Oriental people always look younger than you probably are to me." Claire winced again and Gus, observing this response, rolled her eyes so she could be seen to be on the right side of political correctness, too. Amanda didn't notice this by-play as she was continuing to regard both boys carefully. "I guess I'd have to say that he was more like your age, Gerry, er Gerald. Or maybe even older."

"I know guys who are 22, 23, even 25 at the college so that would be possible," Gerald said.

Dan made a comment at this point. "That puts a whole new spin on things, doesn't it? You've been focusing on the black car, but what if more than one person is involved? Claire, you told me that the boy who was killed was likely selling drugs at the school but he was quite old for a high school student. What if he was a college student? Did anybody see his obituary? It might have said something there?"

"I will check with Sergeant Crombie tomorrow," Claire said. "That is definitely worth following up, Dan. Thank you."

Marian timidly raised her voice at that point. "May I say something?"

Claire nodded her head and Marian went on. "I'm wondering if those people who run that café have any teenaged or adult children? You *said* they were middle-aged."

"Wow!" Claire said. "I never even thought of that!" She looked meaningfully at Tia, and Jimmy saw the look and scowled.

Tia spoke then. "I'm still cleaning at the café. Both Claire and Jimmy asked me to stop, but as we have such few leads I didn't think I could break that connection. Wu Chen and his wife, Yeung Lan, are the only possible connection we have to whatever happened to Sam. Yeung Lan has asked and continues to ask if I'll consider cleaning her house and I'm thinking that's the only possible way we're going to be able to answer Marian's question, which seems to be an important one."

"Oh, no. You're not going to do *that!"* Jimmy expostulated. "*Too* dangerous!" He turned to Claire and snarled. "I knew right away that was what you were getting at. I swear sometimes I think you're deliberately trying to get her killed!"

Everybody shuffled uncomfortably and Dan started to get to his feet as if to say something, but Claire waved at him to sit down. She sat down herself and put her head in her hands and Tia went over and put her arm around her, awkwardly, as she was still standing. Then she turned to the group and took over the meeting as if nothing had happened.

"Just for the record, I'd like to recap what Claire has done for this group to date. And there's nothing much in it for her when you get right down to it. Her own profoundly disabled daughter is sitting at home with an assistant as we speak and gets nothing out of this whole effort. True, Claire is now getting paid a modest salary but it's far less than she could get if she took her decorating business half as seriously as she has taken this and she could do that now that she finally has reliable help for Jessie. I'd like to just mention for any of you who don't know that Claire was really good at her profession and won several important awards. More importantly, she has a host of satisfied customers and could practically run her business on referrals alone if she had only the chance to focus on it.

Now all of this might seem to have nothing to do with the issue at hand, but what it points to is the kind of drive and commitment Claire has for this project—which she practically single-handedly made happen in the first place." Tia turned to Jimmy at that point and asked, "Or have you forgotten, Jimmy?"

Tia went on speaking. "With all Claire's drive, however, and with all her ingenuity and with whatever *I* was able to bring to the table we're still at a dead end. And this is not just about solving some intriguing little puzzle I might remind you. This is about Roscoe's *life.* Now, I ask you. Where do you *suggest* we go from here? Because if you have any better ideas than what we've come up with today, I'm sure both Claire and I would be most happy to hear them."

Nobody said anything for a moment and then Marian started slowly clapping. Everybody joined in and Claire raised her head and smiled but there were tears in her eyes, tears of exhaustion and worry and frustration and hurt, and it was obvious that she had permanently ceded the floor to Tia. Mario walked over to her quietly and shyly handed her a couple of Kleenex he'd grabbed from a box on the coffee table. Claire reached over to him and gave him a long hug.

Roscoe's dad Fuji got up at that point. "I think my wife and I need to say something to all of you people. First, we are of course very, very grateful for all your care and concern for our son. Second, we want to say that, apart from this unfortunate matter, we have never seen Roscoe happier than he has been since the home was established—and we owe that mostly to Claire and we know it. Tia, we don't want you to put your own life in danger for Roscoe. We agree with Jimmy there. And I don't know how you think you could even do that and risk leaving Mario an orphan. You are clearly a rational person so what makes you think you could safely go into that house and what would you do once you got there anyway?"

Fuji sat down at this point and Tia stood up. "Believe me, Fuji, I'm not interested in taking any more risks. Even at the café, I'm just in a holding pattern. I'm cleaning, not actively investigating, just to keep the connection with them going. It's quite clear that they regard me, or at least my cleaning skills, very highly at this point and that they appreciate the fact that I've gone the extra mile for them."

Tia stopped herself suddenly. She was beginning to sound like Claire with all her clichés and outdated analogies. Then she went on. "I think I have built their confidence and trust in me. On one or two occasions already, Lan has confided little snippets about her discontent with how Wu Chen wants to run things in the café. She told me, for example, that he was the one who wanted to bring in the sunflower oil from Mexico because it's cold pressed and supposed to be so good, but our own canola oil grown right here in Alberta has an even better health profile than sunflower oil and it would be much cheaper to use. They go through a lot of oil at the café with all that frying."

Claire thought about this and started to say something, but was interrupted by Thomas, Randy's younger son at this point. "Sofu Fuji says that guy who was killed was selling drugs at our school. I *have* heard people talk about getting drugs there. And I also heard that a student died of a drug overdose in November. He was one of the seniors and nobody official is talking about it. Maybe I could dig around and find out if there is a new supplier and who he is."

"No!" his grandmother, Yuna, said. "You stay safe––and don't talk to *anybody* there about Roscoe. They should not know that you even *know* him!"

Fuji looked at her reprovingly. "You expect other people to take risks for Roscoe but not his oikko …nephew?"

Claire interjected again. "Whether Thomas is related or not is not the point here. He's sixteen, a minor. It would be totally irresponsible to allow him to get involved. One person has been killed already."

Thomas sat back sulkily and said nothing. Tia looked at him and recognized something in his expression. She had the feeling he was going to do exactly what he felt he needed to do whatever anyone said. Therefore, he needed a little guidance. "Claire makes a good point," she said to Thomas. "There's real danger here. You should be very careful not to let *anyone* at school know you have *any* connection with Roscoe or that you even know about Sam's murder. If you *ever* talk to anyone there about drugs you should give the impression that it's because *you* want them for yourself, and that you don't care at all who's doing the actual selling. But, of course, you should really just stay clear of this whole mess and say nothing to anybody!"

Thomas gave her a quick secret smile and nodded his head slightly which Tia took to mean he got the message on procedure but was not going to be deterred from trying to get some helpful information.

Gerald, not to be outdone, jumped in at this point. "If drugs are in the high school then for sure they're in the college. And I'm an adult so I can make my own decisions—but I get the point about caution, not asking pointed questions and not letting on about knowing Roscoe Oji. I can also ask around about where I can get hard drugs. It was cocaine you found, wasn't it?" he asked, directing his attention to Tia.

Randy interrupted before Tia could answer. "You will not be doing that while you live under *my* roof! It *is* too dangerous!"

"Uh-huh," was all Gerald said, with a hint of insolence in his voice.

"Okay!" Tia said briskly. "I think that's all we have time for today. You have given us a lot to think about and thank you all very much for coming. I'll type up a summary of our conversation along with a possible action plan and email it out to all of you for any further comments you may have. Please make sure your email address is on the list I put out on the table and please come and enjoy some cake and coffee before you leave."

Chapter 32: An Action Plan Emerges

Tia had the meeting summary typed up and sent out by the following Tuesday. She listed each idea put forward, the person who proposed it and the responsibility they had volunteered to take. She then asked everyone to look over the list and rate the ideas in order of potential value and make suggestions as to how best they could be implemented.

Tia sent the group email at 7 p.m. and at 8 p.m., she left for her regular cleaning stint at the restaurant. She had been making it a point to go in earlier in order to build confidence with the Wus, as she referred to them collectively. Lan was still there and greeted her warmly. "You haven't changed your mind about cleaning for me by any chance?" she asked.

Tia looked at her, took a breath but then responded in the negative. She just couldn't go through another bad scene with Jimmy. But as she worked through her tasks that evening, she had a hard time concentrating. She just felt sad and wrong and angry. *Jimmy should understand!* she thought.

Meanwhile, Claire was at her own home writing out a list of rules for amateur investigators which she then planned to send out to all the people who'd attended their meeting:

1. If the police can do it and they will do it, don't even try.

2. Guilty people are suspicious people. They will read into innocent statements even when there is nothing there, never mind when you are trying to get

something out of them. Be very careful what you say and to whom you say it.

3. Never try to con a con. They are way ahead of you and will see right through you and then *you* will be at risk.

4. Don't talk to any possible suspect any more than absolutely necessary. Every word increases your risk. And forget about the folksy touch. They will smell a rat right away.

5. If you are on a trail don't confide in anyone—except us.

Once she'd sent the email, Claire felt a bit better but she was still worried, especially about Randy's sons. It seemed to her that the whole family shared a collective guilt about having put Roscoe in an institution those many years ago even though Randy, the younger brother of Roscoe, had not even been born at the time. And guilt can make you do strange things and take unnecessary risks. Claire decided she'd have a word with Yuna, the boy's mother, to put her on the alert and that was about all she could do at this point.

That evening, Claire and Tia met for coffee to discuss what else could be done to find the black car. "You know," Tia said, "it's April now and we're having a warm spring so far. People are starting to walk around more. If we worked as a team, we could systematically walk the streets without it being apparent what we are doing. Then when we identified a likely car, Gus and Amanda could walk over and have a look at it."

"That's an idea," Claire agreed, and started making a list of the people they could ask to participate.

"What about asking Roscoe's parents?" Tia asked. "*They* are not working during the day and I know they are feeling badly about the rest of us trying so hard to protect their son while they're doing nothing. They could drive over and park their car somewhere and then just walk around the streets like they were just another older couple out for a walk."

"Well," Claire said. "It's a good idea in principle and I agree that we should try to get them involved in some way. But we have to remember who we are dealing with. He's looking for Roscoe and is going to be on the lookout for anybody Asian in the neighborhood so he would be quicker to notice them than somebody else—and we don't want him to know that we're actively looking for him."

"Well, *who* then? It's going to look funny for young people to be out walking around leisurely during the day."

"I think the logical people to do it are Gus and Amanda. After all, they're the ones who know exactly what the black car looks like and they're of an age for it to seem quite normal to be seen strolling around regularly. Also, they're itching to be more involved."

Chapter 33: The Search for Answers

Gus and Amanda were clearly delighted when Claire asked them to undertake the walking task. They walked in the days and they walked in the evenings. They walked down streets and they walked up alleys. And they peered through garage windows to check out the cars inside whenever they had a chance to do so without being seen.

But after two weeks of this, they had nothing of substance to report. And the car had stopped coming in the mornings. It was as if the driver now knew what he needed and was just lurking somewhere, waiting for his chance to attack Roscoe.

Tia was expressing all this to Jimmy one night and ended by saying, "I don't know why Gus and Amanda can't find that car if the driver really does live in the neighborhood."

Mario was studying nearby and overheard this comment. "Why do you think he lives in the neighborhood? If he found where Roscoe lives by following the handicap bus, then he could live anywhere on the bus route. He could be a couple of miles away!"

Tia considered this and nodded slowly. "Yes, you could be right, Mario. Trying to track him down could be a rather hopeless task then, I guess."

Mario returned to his studying and Tia turned back to Jimmy. "I guess the only lead we have left is the café and now Yeung Lan's house." Roscoe *did* recognize somebody in the café that time and ran away, so we know there is a connection."

Jimmy just shook his head. "I don't like you there. What if she's in on it? Remember what happened the last time you cleaned house for a killer?"

Tia took his hand. "I promise I'll be very careful," she said. "But I have to do this. There's no other way left."

The next evening, Tia made sure to get to the store before Yeung Lan left, and she casually mentioned to her that one of her regulars was leaving for a two-month long visit with her daughter who had a term position teaching at the University of Colorado in Denver. As of now, Tia had a temporary Wednesday morning opening for that time period if Yeung Lan was still interested in her services.

"That is good!" Yeung Lan exclaimed, with more than the usual level of Chinese enthusiasm. "Can you come tomorrow morning? It is Wednesday." It was agreed and the next morning, Tia turned up at the home of Wu Chen and Yeung Lan at 9:15 a.m. She asked to see the cleaning equipment and experienced her usual level of disappointment at the inadequate vacuum cleaner, limp, grey floor mop and motley collection of cleaning supplies. Fortunately, she had anticipated this and the trunk of her car was loaded with all she would need, including her own high performance vacuum. Tia explained that, just as at the café, she was more comfortable working with her own cleaning materials and proceeded to haul them in and get to work.

By noon, the carpets were as clean and groomed as they could get without shampooing, the furniture was dusted and oiled and polished, light fixtures had been cleaned and bulbs replaced where necessary, visible dirt had been spot cleaned from the walls and the baseboards and hard floors had been thoroughly vacuumed and washed. As difficult as it was to read Yeung Lan's expression, Tia thought she detected a note of awe in it and sat down gratefully when Yeung Lan offered her some tea.

They visited a bit and then Tia heard the front door opening. She thought it was Wu Chen returning but instead a young man entered the kitchen where they were sitting. Yeung Lan introduced him as her nephew, explaining that her sister-in-law had died some years ago and the young man Gen and his older brother, Denin, had been adopted by them. Currently, Wu Gen was attending the local high school and Wu Denin was in the near-by junior college studying computer programming. But he spent very little time at home, Yeung Lan informed Tia, preferring to hang out with his friends.

When Tia loaded her cleaning materials in her car, she noticed a bicycle leaning carelessly against the fence that had not been there when she arrived. After a furtive look back at the windows facing the yard, she dropped her vacuum cleaner and took a couple of quick pictures with her cell phone. She then drove home and went directly to Amanda's house next door to show her and Gus the pictures.

"It was that color!" Gus exclaimed. "And I remember it had a carrier on the back like that."

Chapter 34: Down But Not Out

It was Friday afternoon and Claire and Roscoe were heading home from the Art Centre. Sarah Hughes had arranged for a special guest speaker that afternoon, a photographer named Ed Slant, who talked about some of the techniques he used to take pictures. Ed spoke in very clear and simple terms and showed the students many examples of his work. They all seemed to enjoy his presentation in their own way, but Roscoe was clearly the most engaged, asking several questions and becoming excited when he understood how the zoom lens worked to allow Ed to get the beautiful, close up picture of a blue jay eating berries off a mountain ash tree. Roscoe had developed a sudden interest in photography a few months earlier and Claire was trying hard to encourage it.

They had taken the Light Rail Transit, Edmonton's version of the subway, to the Centre that day, because it was the fastest way to get downtown and because Claire was anxious to help Roscoe become as independent as possible and not always rely on DATS for getting places. As the train tickets were good for 90 minutes, Claire suggested they stop off at the Corona station on the way back and pick up some books she had ordered at Audrey's Book Store, the main independent book store remaining open in Edmonton.

Roscoe had agreed. They had picked up the books and were now approaching the Metro steps to board the LRT again when Claire suddenly realized they had a problem. Roscoe had a real fear of going down steps although he could go up them easily enough. The cement staircase leading to the Corona station was particularly deep and dark.

Roscoe took one look at the steps and began to shake his head. "No. No steps. I scared."

"Come on, Roscoe," Claire cajoled. "You can do it. These are the same steps you came up an hour ago."

Not down. Down too hard!"

Claire took him by the hand and said with less patience than usual, "Come on. Just do it. We'll be down in a minute."

Roscoe seemed to understand there was no winning but he jerked his hand away, moved to the stair rail and prepared to walk down backwards.

But Claire had had enough and she was also tired of the curious onlookers who were watching the show. "You're not a baby and you're not an old man. Go down the middle of the stairs and go down properly. You can do it at home, so I know you can do it here!" She took his hand back and guided him to the centre of the stairs. "Let's go!" she said. "If we don't go soon, our tickets won't be any good and then we'll have to buy new ones and you'll have to pay for them. That will use up your treat money for the week and I thought you wanted to have a piece of coconut cream pie tomorrow at that new restaurant we found!"

Roscoe said nothing, but he jerked his hand away again and prepared to walk slowly down the middle of the steps. But just as his right foot reached down to the first step, a bicycle came out of nowhere and rammed into him! Roscoe pitched forward with both arms spread wide and flung out in front of him. The impact had been so hard that he seemed for a moment to be almost flying through the air like Superman. The moment seemed frozen in time and the people near the subway opening just stopped and stared, unable to do anything.

Fortunately, there had been a recent lull in LRT traffic and the only people on the subway steps at that point were two tall teenaged boys walking down in tandem a few steps below Roscoe. They turned when they heard the impact and grasped hands. Roscoe catapulted into them and they buckled somewhat but managed to hold on by each grabbing onto a side rail. Once they'd regained their equilibrium, each of them supported Roscoe under an arm and managed to shift him upright and turn him around. Then they half dragged him back up the stairs.

Onlookers cheered and Claire was weeping openly. On shaking legs, she staggered towards the boys and Roscoe and wrapped her arms around all three of them as if she would never let them go. Two men came forward, gently pried her away and helped the three over to a nearby bench with Roscoe sitting in the middle supported by one boy on each side. The boys were pale and shaking and clearly suffering from a drop in blood sugar from the incredible adrenalin rush they had just experienced and Claire noticed for the first time that they were actually twins in their late teens. Huddled between them, Roscoe looked little and strangely old. He was unresponsive, appearing to be frozen with fear or shock or both.

Several of the onlookers hovered around and a policeman approached as someone had had the presence of mind to call 911. He quickly took names and contact information from all of them and then asked the group in general, including Claire and the boys, if anyone had seen anything.

"It was a blue bike. I know *that!*" a middle-aged woman said. "He came from *that* direction," and she pointed south towards the river. "Then he just wove right across the street through the traffic and took off east down the sidewalk."

"I just caught a glimpse of him," said one of the men who'd helped the boys and Roscoe over to the bench, but I'm pretty sure it was a guy, a young guy in his twenties maybe—and maybe Asian. I just got a quick impression."

Others joined in then, agreeing or disagreeing with one or both of these observations. The policeman did his best to write everything down but in the end he gave up and asked five of them to come down to the station the next day and make separate statements. Then he asked the boys what they'd seen but their total focus had been on Roscoe. They had seen nobody else, not even the onlookers or Claire.

When the policeman finally left, Claire asked the boys if they could help her get Roscoe to the coffee shop she'd spied a half-block south and if they would please allow her to buy them some hot chocolate and pastry as a thank you for the wonderful thing they had done for him. They nodded their heads mutely and stood up. Each boy took Roscoe by an arm, and started trudging down the street.

The four of them sat down at a corner table in Mondo Café with hot chocolate and warm cinnamon buns. Claire asked the boys to tell her again what they had seen and how they had managed that wonderful joint rescue act but they just sat there with their hands wrapped around their cups drinking slowly. Roscoe was drinking his cocoa with a spoon and his whole hand was shaking so half of it spilled back on the table. He was eating his cinnamon bun in big bites and it did not seem like he was even aware that he was eating. Halfway through their chocolate, the boys began to talk in response to Claire's questions. They were indeed twins, identical twins, nineteen-years-old and just completing their first year of university in mechanical engineering. In that moment of crisis, their brains had worked in parallel. They had experienced this before as is sometimes the case with twins.

Each had somehow known exactly what to do and what the other would be doing. In fact, there had been no other being for them at that moment in time. It was as if they were one unit, one body. The arms that had joined together to stop Roscoe's fall now hung limply, close to their sides, because the full impact of Roscoe's weight at that speed had left them badly bruised.

Chapter 35: The Circle Grows

Dan came to drive Claire and Roscoe home a short while after this revelation, but Claire was not willing to let the two boys walk out of their lives. Before they parted that evening, Claire extracted a promise that they would come to a special thank you dinner to meet Roscoe's parents and uncle and roommates and his other friends.

This dinner happened a week later with everyone pitching in to make it a memorable feast. Chairs had been pushed back and portable tables brought in covered with tablecloths from several different households. Tia's parents even joined them for a chance to meet the wonder boys, bringing with them a huge pot of Italian-style roasted chicken, 'Pollo alla Cacciatoria.' Gus brought her Swedish meatballs, one of the few dishes she could reliably make and others brought a variety of salads, desserts and even some homemade bread provided by Hilda. Roscoe's parents turned up with an industrial-sized platter of sushi and sashimi for starters, and his uncle came along with a bottle of Saki under his arm that he warmed and served with the Japanese starters in Mavis' tiny plastic medication cups, the perfect size for this potent drink.

The gathering enjoyed a spectacular meal and only at the end of it did they ask the boys to recount their story of how they had responded to Roscoe's fall. Roscoe was wide-eyed listening to this because the experience had been so traumatic for him that he had largely blocked it out of his consciousness. He turned to them when they'd finished recounting the experience and said. "You *save* me. You my brothers now…blood brothers," and he looked at Daisuke for confirmation. They had obviously been having this discussion.

Meanwhile, Terry and Teddy Linehan were entranced with this new community and the interesting characters involved. They asked how it had started and Claire and Tia regaled them with tales of the various adventures that had occurred along the way. Both boys shyly asked if they ever needed volunteers and the grateful rcsponse was *yes*!

Claire looked at Tia and Tia gave her a slight nod so Claire then told them about all the things that had been happening to Roscoe since witnessing Sam's murder and their need to find out who was behind it. The boys were outraged and immediately offered to help. They said they would keep their ears tuned in at the University for any chatter about drug contacts there just in case there was a connection. They lived too far from Roscoe's home to be any use in terms of watching out for a blue bike or a lurking black car.

As Tia and Jimmy were crossing the street to go home from this special evening, Tia commented with a new note of certainty in her voice, "I'm sorry, Jimmy, but if this mystery is going to be solved, I have a feeling it's going to be up to me. I'm going to find out Lan's schedule, and make an excuse about having to come on whatever day she's out of the house because of a change in my own schedule so I'll be free to really snoop around. I can't do much while she's there."

Tia braced herself to counter what she was sure would be the loud objections from Jimmy but he just looked at her sorrowfully and said softly, "I know. Claire has the big ideas but when it comes to actually getting the job done, it seems to always come down to you. That humble house cleaner routine really works to get on the inside. Please, please just be careful and if there's any way, any way at *all* I can help to protect you, please let me. I can't stand to think of you in danger but it's just terrible to see what Roscoe is going through and to never know what is going to happen to him next."

"Thank you, Jimmy," Tia responded gratefully. "Believe me, I'll be super cautious—but *something* has to be done!"

Chapter 36: Tia *Really* Cleans House!

The party had been Saturday night and the next day Tia phoned Lan to let her know that she was not available the coming Wednesday morning, but could do her cleaning that Tuesday morning. She had noted on the reminder list that Lan kept on her fridge that Lan had a 10 o'clock doctor's appointment for that day and was going out for lunch with a friend after that. That should give her about three hours to snoop while she cleaned, she reasoned.

Lan agreed to this change after a moment's hesitation, only asking Tia to leave the door locked behind her by using the lock button when she left. Tia arrived early that day and began cleaning vigorously in order to get as much done in as short a time as possible. She also made a point of leaving cleaning supplies all over the house so that if somebody came home and caught her unaware, she'd have a logical reason for being wherever she was at that point in time.

As soon as Lan was safely out of the house and her car was gone from the drive, Tia propped a dust mop outside the door and began attacking the first of the two nephews' bedrooms. It was somewhat disappointing in a way. There were no dirty clothes under the bed, no giant dust bunnies and no masses of mismatched objects cluttered around. There was only a surface layer of dirt although the bathroom the two young men shared required a little more work.

Tia went about her tasks briskly and automatically, counting the time until she could get to her primary task of snooping. By eleven o'clock, she'd been through the whole house and was waiting for the washing machine to finish. Tia checked the windows and ensured that both doors were locked and then she started systematically going through drawers and closets. But she found nothing of any interest. Tia scrutinized the inside of closet walls with the powerful flashlight she had brought. No luck.

Tia checked under mattresses, felt for loose floorboards and even went through the freezer compartment in the fridge since there was no separate freezer just in case some clever person had decided to hide incriminating material in that format. In fact, she was so busy rooting around in this heavily packed freezer compartment that she didn't hear the door open and finally turned around to find Wu Chen staring at her with a quizzical look on his face. Tia hastily replaced the freezer items she was holding on a tray with one hand while she had been systematically searching them with the other and then closed the door and scrambled down from the chair she was standing on.

"I was just checking to see if there was any freezer burnt food here and whether or not I needed to defrost the freezer compartment while waiting for the washer to finish downstairs," she explained but she couldn't prevent the red flush on her face.

Wu Chen looked at her skeptically and Tia excused herself to check on the washing that fortunately was finished—and, even more fortunately, required hanging rather than machine drying. She brought the basket upstairs and quickly hung the clothes up on the rack that Lan had provided for that purpose after placing the rack in an airy spot.

"Okay!" Tia said brightly. "That's it for today," and she quickly made her escape.

Chapter 37: Another Tack

Tia discussed the matter with Jimmy, Gus and Claire that evening. Amanda was at her lady's group, which she'd been urging Gus to join and which Gus was resisting. They were sitting together in Jimmy's and Tia's living room and Mario was doing homework at the dining room table.

"There's nothing strange in that house; nothing you would not expect to find for two young men busy with their schoolwork and a middle-aged couple busy with their jobs. If they're up to something they are *not* bringing it home with them," Tia groaned.

Nobody said anything for a moment and then Mario interjected his thought. Maybe it's not them at all. There are lots of blue bicycles. I was counting them in the bike rack at school today and about one out of every three was blue. Maybe it's not them at all!"

Jimmy grinned at Mario. "Always thinking, kid, aren't you?"

Mario allowed himself a small grin in return. He was always happy for any positive sign in the relationship-building project with Jimmy he had privately set for himself.

The others just looked at him and then Claire said, "well, if it's not them then we're back to square one."

Tia added, rather severely, "I know you're concerned about Roscoe, Mario, but I don't want you to do *anything* that will make you stand out and standing there staring at bicycles could definitely be seen as suspicious behavior by whoever is doing this."

It's just an elementary school, mom. The oldest kid there is twelve!"

"And who says kids have the same taste in bike colors as adults, any way?" Gus offered.

"That's a point," Jimmy agreed. "But where do we go from here?"

"Well, I'll tell you what Amanda and I are going to do," Gus expounded. "We're going to go for a nice leisurely walk tomorrow which just happens to take us by the high school bike racks and we'll check out the number of blue bikes—and the type. Remember, Amanda saw the bike. Then, if we have the energy, we'll walk all the way to the college and do the same thing. If not, we'll probably do it the day after."

Claire weighed in then. "Roscoe is in really bad shape since this latest incident. He even wet the bed last night and he hasn't done that in ages. He said he was afraid to get up, even though he needed to, and then he just fell asleep and it happened. And he's refusing to go anywhere on the LRT. He says the bad guy must have followed him there and maybe he's right. I don't understand how that guy on the bike knew we would be at the Corona LRT station. We didn't even decide to go to the bookstore until we were actually on the way back from the Art Centre."

"Maybe that's a clue," Mario said excitedly. "Maybe he works there!"

"Or," added Jimmy, "maybe he comes with one of the clients. You mentioned that some of them don't come on their own, Claire. Do the assistants stay in the class or do they go off somewhere?"

"No, they're obliged to stay there." The students who require a mandatory escort on DATS either have serious behavior problems or else they're medically fragile and cannot travel unaccompanied. In either case, the assistants are obliged to stay nearby when they're at the Art Centre."

Claire thought for a moment and then added, her face flushed with excitement, "It's true that any one of them could have overheard us and some of them have been coming with the same clients for as long as we've been there. In fact, one of them could have overheard me that first day when I was explaining to the director what had happened to Roscoe."

"You need to find out about them, Claire. And, *for once,* this isn't something Tia can do," Jimmy exclaimed.

"I'll ask the director about the three who were there the first day we went. I'm trying to think if any of them were also there last time, the day of the incident. I remember that first day there were two guys and a girl. The students come with different assistants sometimes but I think it would have to be one of them who were there that first day."

"Why?" Mario asked.

"How else would they know what had happened?"

"They probably all work in group homes which means they work with others. They could have gone back and talked about it and it could be another worker in the home."

"You're right, Mario!" Claire groaned. "So how are we ever going to figure it out?"

"Maybe the director keeps some personal information on them, including their addresses. It would likely have to be somebody who lives in this area, don't you think?" Tia offered.

"I don't know," Claire groaned. "It's all so complicated."

"Start with the director. But make sure you're not overheard this time," Jimmy advised.

Chapter 38: A New Direction or a Dead End?

Claire arranged to meet with the director of the East Winds Rising Art Centre the very next day. Sarah Hughes welcomed Claire and took her to an office closed off from the main room of the Centre that she had not seen before. Claire let Sarah in more fully on what had been happening, including the attack on Roscoe on the way home from the Centre and she was predictably horrified.

"Do you think it could have any connection with anybody here?" Sarah asked, and Claire was relieved that she hadn't needed to raise this possibility herself.

"It seems so unlikely that I'd never even considered it until this latest incident. But then I got to thinking that a lot of assistants do come with the adult students and we *did* talk about this together in the big room a couple of times including the very first time we came. We *could* have been overheard."

"That's true, I guess, but I just can't imagine who could be involved. Most of these assistants have come here from other countries, largely from the Philippines or from various conflicted countries in Africa. They're just struggling to survive and to get a foothold and to feed their families. I don't see them as having either the connections or the energies to pursue something as nefarious as drug smuggling and to then cover it up with murder."

"I feel the same," Claire sighed. "But *somebody* has been doing this—and this last incident points towards a connection here. I was trying to remember who was here that very first time that Roscoe and I came because I believe that's the only time I really talked to you about the murder he witnessed and how it was affecting him. As I recall, you introduced me to Hank, Mike and Betty that day. They all had helpers with them, I believe, but I don't remember their names. I know the people who come with them now but I don't know if it was the same back then. It was several months ago and Roscoe and I were both pretty upset at the time."

"Well, I should be able to help you with that. Those three always come with the same assistants and I do have some basic information on file about them. We require that for security purposes. What would you need to know?"

"I guess I'd like to know if any of them live near the cafe where this all started. And also if they all work full time because whoever killed Sam and is continuing to target Roscoe must have some flexible hours at his disposal."

Sarah checked her files, explaining that she could not give Claire direct access for confidentiality reasons but, given the seriousness of the situation, would share the two pieces of information Claire had requested. Claire returned to the big room and sat down with a cup of coffee and a cookie to wile away the time while she waited for Sarah to peruse her files. Fifteen minutes later, Sarah came back.

"Jarred has been working with Hank for over a year. He emigrated from the Congo to Montreal two years before that and I have references on file for him from the Extended Care Hospital he worked for there as well as from his current employer and nothing stands out. Both say he's reliable, hard working and gets along well with the clients. He lives in the northeast part of the city—in Beverly—and the house he works in is also in the northeast. He works there full-time on a rotating schedule of day, afternoon and night shifts, and he has a wife and two little girls. I recall talking to the supervisor at his agency when she was arranging for him to bring Hank here and she said he often tried to pick up extra shifts. His girls are quite young and his wife does not work outside the home so it's all on him. Also, she speaks very little English so her job prospects aren't good unless she can improve her language skills. He often seems stressed and preoccupied but he *is* good to Hank as you have probably noticed."

"I haven't heard him say much. How are his language skills?"

"Functional but limited. French is the language of instruction in the Congo. I don't know why they didn't stay in Montreal. Maybe the job prospects were better here."

Claire had been automatically making notes but he didn't sound like a likely suspect. "What about the other two?"

"Well, Carmina has been working with Betty a couple of years now. She managed to get her work visa renewed and hopes to stay and bring her family over. Like a lot of women coming here from the Philippines she had no choice but to leave young children at home with her husband and parents so she could come here and make money and establish a foothold.

Carmina is quite open and friendly and has talked to me about her situation. I know she sends most of her money home to support them and is just hoping to get landed immigrant status soon so she can bring them over. And you will have noticed that she and Betty get along very well. I don't see her as having the time or energy to get up to any clever tricks and she certainly does not seem to be the type who could commit a murder. Besides, didn't you say that Roscoe talked about a man when it happened?"

"That's true," Claire sighed. "But just to be thorough, can you tell me what part of the city she lives and works in and if she has full time work."

"She's definitely full time and she even has a second job on weekends, she told me. Like I said, her whole goal is to make enough money to be able to bring her family over when she can. She lives in a one room bed-sit downtown and she doesn't drive. She works in the West End and told me she has a forty-minute bus ride everyday for this job but the weekend job is close to where she lives."

"Okay," Claire said resignedly. "I guess we can move on to Mike's worker."

"He's a bit of a different case."

"Oh?" said Claire, her interest quickening. "His English seems pretty good, colloquial, anyways. I was wondering where *he* was from?"

"Farron is Canadian, born right here in Alberta."

Claire raised her eyebrows, trying to figure out how to frame her next question without sounding like she was stereotyping.

"I know what you're thinking. He does look kind of different. He is Native Canadian, but with some Black ancestry as well."

"He doesn't seem to spend much time with Mike when he's here. He seems to spend most of his time on his phone," Claire said cautiously.

It was Sarah's turn to sigh. "I know. And you've probably noticed that indifference with some of the others, too. There certainly is a core group of dedicated workers in this field but many others, and particularly a good number of the Canadians I've seen in this field, seem to act like they're slumming and just marking time until something better comes along.

The Community Living movement started off with such high hopes but workers in the field have never received the same wages, benefits and job security that they enjoyed in the institutions—and strangely enough they don't feel like they have the same status. That appears to demoralize a lot of them and some seem to cover their feelings of failure and inferiority by acting like the clients are beneath them. It's very hard to watch when there's so much important work that needs to be done to give the people they're serving a reasonable quality of life."

Claire silently agreed but she also needed to bring the conversation back on track. "Well, what do you think of Farron in particular?"

"From what I've seen of him, he doesn't strike me as particularly frustrated or bored, more just kind of on the lazy, unmotivated side. He likes to talk and joke with friends on the phone and discuss what they're going to do in their time off which usually involves girls or bars or hockey games or macho movies or a combination of same. I personally don't think he would have either the energy or the self-discipline to get involved in something as dangerous or demanding as drug running––or the chutzpah to actually murder someone."

"No, I don't think so either, from what you've said. And I guess that's *it*: another dead end." Claire's shoulders slumped.

Sarah looked at her sympathetically. "If I can think of anything else I'll let you know. Meanwhile, I really hope you can find a way to convince Roscoe to come back. I thought he was doing well here and beginning to open up with his drawings."

"I know. It's just cruel. Every time he begins to trust a bit and take a step forward something else happens. I don't know what to do to help him. But he does seem to feel safe here. I'll try to convince him to come with me in my car. Maybe he'll feel confident enough to do that."

"That's an idea!" Sarah replied, and with that they parted.

Chapter 39: What To Do Next?

Claire met with Jimmy and Tia and Gus again that evening, a Friday evening, and this time Amanda joined them. Mario was in Wetaskiwin, a small town 70 kilometers south of Edmonton, spending the weekend with his grandparents. Claire reported the disappointing news from the Art Centre to the others and mentioned her idea of asking Roscoe if he'd travel with her by car there. Everyone thought that was a good idea but, like Claire, felt discouraged by the lack of any viable leads.

After a few moments had passed when it had become obvious that nobody had any great new ideas to suggest, Tia spoke up. "I know we're all in a bad spot here wondering what's going to happen and it's really put a damper on all our lives, but I actually have some good news to report on a different matter," and she gave Jimmy a secret smile.

"You're pregnant!" Gus burst out.

"No-o-o. That would be a bit premature, don't you think? However, what I have to tell you does relate in a certain way."

"Well, get on with it then!" Gus demanded, in a blustering effort to cover her faux pas.

"I heard from the priest today. My annulment has come through. Jimmy and I just have to go for a few marriage preparation sessions with him and we'll be free to legally marry!"

Jimmy was grinning broadly and Claire rushed over to hug Tia. Gus, not wanting to be left out, awkwardly added to the hug. Amanda, with somewhat more dignity, warmly congratulated Tia and Jimmy while remaining seated and asked when they thought the wedding could take place and where. She recalled that Tia had once mentioned Mexico.

Jimmy spoke then. "We've waited a long time for this and we don't want to wait any longer than necessary. We've already checked with Tia's priest and he has a Saturday opening two weeks from now at two in the afternoon. We just need to be out of there in time for them to prepare for 5 o'clock Mass."

"Two weeks! Where can you find a hall for the reception in two weeks?" Amanda exclaimed.

"If we can't find a hall, we're going to do the reception right here," Jimmy replied.

"You don't have much room."

"We've thought about this," Tia said. "Our home is at the core of the new community that we're building—you and Gus and the people across the street and friends in the neighborhood. Just think about it!" she added, enthusiastically. "This way, we'll have three ovens and three fridges to deal with all the food, assuming you are okay with that, Amanda?"

"Of course! Anything I can do to help. Are you going to have it catered or will we do the cooking ourselves?"

"I was hoping to do it ourselves. I can't see the point in spending a bundle just to show off. We just want to share the occasion with close friends and family and I don't imagine there will be more than 30 or 40 of us. After all, Jimmy and I were each married once already so this should be a low-key affair in my opinion," Tia replied. She added as an after thought, "It will be mid-May by then and if we have to have it here, we should be able to spill over into the back yard. We could set up a big tent out there with a heater in it and some lights strung up."

"It should be lovely!" Claire said. "And I think we all need something to celebrate at this point after all the worry we've been through. I propose we just put our investigation on hold for a couple of weeks and concentrate on keeping Roscoe safe and helping you prepare for the wedding in any way we can. I want this to be a really special and perfect day for both of you!"

Tia hugged her and announced to everyone that they had cake and champagne to celebrate the upcoming celebration. She then brought out her latest concoction, a Boston cream cake piled high with whipping cream and dark chocolate shavings and with a rich custard filling. Everyone had a glass of champagne to toast the happy couple and then settled into the cake with coffee and tea to wash it down. But one person, Jimmy, was thinking that this home wedding plan was not the greatest idea he'd ever heard.

Chapter 40: Oh Happy Days!

Roscoe agreed to return to the Art Centre but Claire cut his days there down to twice a week. Claire drove Roscoe back and forth to the Centre and remained close to him during their visits, worrying even when he went to the bathroom alone.

Much of the remaining time was spent planning the wedding and everyone was very excited. As only close friends and family were to be invited, it was not as complicated to organize as a larger wedding would have been and everyone in their little group wanted to help with providing the food. A special meeting was arranged at Jimmy's and Tia's house to organize the details.

Amanda declared that she and Gus were buying and preparing a huge baron of beef, enough to feed all of the 40 guests Tia and Jimmy had finally settled on. Claire looked fearfully at Aunt Gus, knowing how limited her culinary skills were, but Amanda saw the look and was quick to assure Claire that *she* would be doing the cooking.

"Don't forget the horseradish!" Jimmy requested. "I am really looking forward to it. That's *my* kind of food!"

"Well, you better not let my mother hear you say that," Tia warned, laughingly. "She's bringing two huge pans of her special lasagna!"

Tia, the cake specialist, was making her own wedding cake. "I know I can do it better than anyone else so why leave it to chance?" was all she would say on that subject.

"Hilda and I are bringing out special Pineapple Charlotte for dessert, light enough to complement the cake without overshadowing it," Marion declared.

"And we're bringing a fancy Japanese tofu and vegetable dish to feed the non-meat eaters in the crowd," Roscoe's mom, Yuna, added.

"Better make lots," Jimmy suggested. "I have a feeling many of the meat eaters will be horning in on it!"

The wedding service would be in Tia's home church of St. Andrew, the church she'd gone to as a child. Father Giacomo, the priest who'd helped her work through the annulment process, would be officiating. The reception would be at the newly renovated Royal Gardens Community Hall that Jimmy, after an all day marathon involving futile calls to a dozen other establishments, had managed to reserve for the evening. As it happened, this was also the hall closest to their home and it was agreed that they could have full use of its kitchen facilities and cater the meal themselves.

Claire hired several of the female assistants who worked part-time at the group home to serve the meal. Everyone who could fit it into their schedule had agreed as they were anxious to be a part of this celebration and to observe Mavis, Bill and Roscoe in that environment.

"It looks like everything is falling into place!" Tia said, contentedly, after reporting to the assembled group this part of the planning process.

"What about the wedding and bridesmaid dresses and the mother of the bride dress?" Gus asked.

"We're planning to shop for them next week," Tia replied. "I don't want anything fancy. It's just a waste of money."

"Hmmph!" Gus sniffed. "I think you deserve better than that. As it happens, Amanda and I have been doing some research around town and have found one shop in particular where we think you could find something very appropriate." Actually, there was no 'we.' Gus had insisted Amanda come with her, but Amanda had been utterly bored by the whole process and had complained about her corns constantly. Gus had had no patience for this, declaring that in the interests of beauty, women must sacrifice comfort. That's just how it was!

After visiting five shops, Gus had finally settled on one which had a fresh and interesting selection of gowns for reasonable prices that she thought would suit Tia's taste. She'd tried hard to convince the store owner that if they were buying four or five dresses all at once, they should have a substantial discount, something like 30%. It was a small shop and Gus knew that made the owners more vulnerable. However, Madame Gunne, as she styled herself (aka Annie Gunn) was no pushover and after a good half hour of hard bargaining, she finally agreed to a 15% discount—but *only* if at least four dresses were purchased.

After they'd left the shop, Amanda asked Gus, "How do you know they're all going to go along with this? Isn't it a bit presumptuous to assume you know all their tastes that well?"

"It's not about their tastes. They have the rest of their lives to indulge their tastes. It's about a tasteful wedding party," Gus growled, although secretly she had felt a qualm or two herself. And now she waited nervously for Tia's response.

"Oh, I don't know that that's necessary," Tia said abstractedly, wanting to get on to a discussion of the more important things, like who was actually going to be in the wedding party, but needing to have that discussion in private with Claire.

Claire nudged Tia under the table when she saw the stricken look on her aunt's face. "On the other hand," Tia said, reading the look that Claire telegraphed to her, "maybe that *would* be a good idea. Neither Claire nor I have much fashion sense when it comes to clothes."

"Well," Gus explained, "wedding shops are very busy at this time of the year, so I took the liberty of tentatively making an appointment for 10 o'clock tomorrow morning because this particular shop didn't have another opening until next week. Do you think you and Claire and Mavis and Jessie and your mother could make it then?"

"Short notice, Aunt Gus! You're beginning to sound like me!" Claire said, laughing slightly at her aunt's audacity. "I can say yes for Mavis and Jessie and me but I don't know about Tia and Marisa."

Tia rolled her eyes at this latest intrusion into her busy schedule. "I can probably manage, but I can't speak for my mother. I'll call her now." The call was made and after some discussion with her husband who would be doing the driving, Marisa agreed that they could make it to Tia's house by 9:30 although Alberto was not happy about driving into the city during the morning rush hour.

Once the meeting finished and the others had left, Tia and Claire relaxed with a glass of wine and mulled over a few unsettled issues. Claire raised something that had been bothering her.

"Tia, I can understand why you want to have Mavis as part of the wedding party but I don't get your reasoning for including Bill." Tia's plan had been for Claire and Mavis to stand up for her and Bill and Roscoe to stand up for Jimmy.

"Well, Jimmy is Bill's co-guardian so in a way he's kind of like family, like Mavis. And also Bill sees himself as Mavis' boyfriend more or less and he would expect to be there with her and Marion would expect it."

"I don't agree. The bottom line is this is your special day and Bill is not predictable. He could start chanting or interrupting the priest and really mess things up. Also, it's going to start to look like a funny farm up there."

Tia gasped. "That is the *last* thing I'd have expected someone in *your* position to say!"

"Wolf Wolfensburger, an early proponent of normalization for persons with developmental disabilities, talked about "deviancy juxtaposition." His idea was that when you bring together a number of people with disabilities in the same place, other people can only see the disabilities, not the individuals. I think that might be what's going to happen here and I'm wondering why you're feeling so obligated to include all three of the people from across the street in your wedding party."

"Well, I don't want to exclude anybody."

"You're excluding friends and relatives you've known for years and in some cases your whole life. What about them? What about your cousin, Vinni, for example?"

"Well, that's different."

"Oh, why? Because he's not disabled? What is this, an affirmative action exercise? Have you ever heard of reverse discrimination?"

"I get your point but it's all very confusing. What do you suggest?"

"Well, first of all, I think your wedding party is too large. I agree that you should have Mavis there as your maid of honor."

"No, *you* are my maid of honor. Mavis is a bridesmaid."

"Tia, I think Mavis needs to be your maid of honor and I need to fill the role of Mavis' assistant. I'm going to take her up to the altar and then I'm going to take my place in the aisle seat front row. If she needs me I can get to her quickly. As I see it, Roscoe can be Jimmy's best man. It will make him feel important and good about himself and after all he's been through, that's certainly a good reason for having him in that role. Also, he understands enough to take it seriously and do what he's supposed to do. That's not something we can assume about Bill and you know what? Bill's not even going to care and Marion certainly won't care. She just cares about you and wants your day to go as smoothly as possible."

Tia looked at Claire for a long time. "I guess you're right about Bill and right about Roscoe and Mavis filling those roles, but I feel badly about you. *You* are my best friend, not Mavis. *You* should be up there."

Claire looked at her friend with tears in her eyes. "You know what. I think when we set about organizing three vulnerable people's lives we took on something bigger than ourselves and somehow we're going to have to act the part. I *will* be there, just a few steps away. Our friendship does not need more than that."

And so it was agreed.

Chapter 41: Power Shopping

The next morning found Tia, Claire, Mavis and Tia's mother, Marisa, at the shop at 10 a.m. Claire had decided to send Jessie to school and take a chance on finding the right fit for Jessie's dress on condition that she could exchange it if needed. Annie Gunn agreed as long as the exchange was made the same day. Exchanges and returns of special occasion dresses were not usually allowed for obvious reasons.

Gus had actually picked out what she considered to be the ideal dresses already, keeping in mind her vision of an elegant and harmonious blending of gowns. She had even chosen the sizes and now Gus swallowed nervously and asked Annie to bring out "some of the dresses she and Annie had thought the members of the group might like to consider'."

Annie was enjoying the discomfort she saw in Gus' face, but decided it was in her best interest to help her with this charade. She brought out the wedding gown Gus had chosen first. Tia held it up against herself and looked in the mirror. "It's very nice," she said diplomatically, "but it looks almost white. I'm not sure that's appropriate for a second wedding."

"It's actually a pale cream color," Gus argued, "but let us look at the rest before you decide."

The bridesmaid dresses came out next. They were a similar pattern, simply cut and made from a soft taffeta that seemed to flow over the body. They were just slightly darker than the wedding gown and did not have its overlay of lace. "You see," Gus said defensively.

"You will all be wearing cream!" Claire examined the dresses but all she said was, "I can see that it would be relatively easy to dress Mavis in this and it should not bunch too much in front when she is seated in her wheelchair."

Gus had hoped for more than this, but grimly asked the shop owner to bring out the last dress, the dress for the mother of the bride. "I do have a perfectly good suit I can wear, you know," Marisa said nervously. "Spending all this money for something I'll probably wear only once seems very wasteful."

"Wait until you see it," Gus said tersely.

Annie came out then, carrying a fawn-colored two-piece suit, together with a classically-cut silk blouse in a lighter cream color that complemented Tia's gown. Marisa, despite a lifetime of being practical, could not stop a sharp inhalation of breath as she saw the simple and dignified grace of the combination. Gus allowed herself a small grin and felt some of her tension ebb away.

Next came the try-ons and some size adjustments. Because of the forgiving waistline of the skirt, Marisa actually needed a smaller size than Gus had chosen for her and when she came out of the change room in her outfit, Gus, Tia, Annie and Claire all looked at her in awe. Marisa, normally somewhat dumpy and matronly in appearance, looked truly svelte and elegant and very much the mother of the bride in the classic, coordinated and slimming outfit Gus had chosen for her. She admired herself from various angles and everyone could see that she was very pleased with the effect.

One down, Gus thought gleefully.

The next task was to bring Mavis into the largest change room and lift her gently onto the floor so they could dress her in the matching bridesmaid dress that Claire now had on. Finally, the task was accomplished and Mavis had been placed back in her chair with the dress tucked in discretely at the waist so as not to bunch up in front of her. Tia exited the change room so she could observe their entrance from a proper perspective and when Claire pushed Mavis out with both of them dressed alike and looking elegant Tia could not hold back her tears. "You're both beautiful!" she exclaimed. "I could not ask for a more elegant wedding party."

With the three women in their respective gowns framed behind her in the mirror, as cleverly organized by Gus and Annie, now working together, Tia studied her own reflection carefully. This was not the dress she would have picked, but to be honest she did not know what she would have chosen. Geared as she was to the practical, she'd never given herself permission to develop an aesthetic sense. Now she turned gently from side to side and could not help feeling a little thrill. She wasn't so uncovered as to be vamp-like nor was the dress so whitish as to be implausibly virginal looking. These concerns being laid to rest, she was able to really look at herself and what she saw was a young, attractive woman who many men might find quite appealing. She thought she could live with that.

Claire next searched for a dress for Jessie who was to be the flower girl. Claire had idly envisioned some bright pink concoction but the color palate Gus had dictated meant her search was now limited to cream She did rebel a bit, finding a white dress with tiny salmon-colored roses sprinkled over the pleated voile bodice and see-through skirt which had a very light, cream-colored taffeta underskirt beneath it. And the long back zipper would make it relatively easy to pull on over Jessie's stiff arms, always an important consideration.

While all this was happening, Jimmy's task during his lunch hour was to pick up the wedding license from

City Hall. He also had set himself another task to accomplish, the details of which he was not sharing with Tia just yet.

Chapter 42: The Wedding Finally Happens

At 7 a.m. on May 15, Claire peaked out her bedroom window and groaned. The air was misty and there were some clouds overhead. What about Tia's dress? They better stuff the floor of her father's car full of tissue paper so Tia would not arrive at the church with the bottom of her dress soiled. Fortunately, they had plenty of it left over from the way the dresses had been so carefully packed to prevent them from being crushed. Claire got up, made some coffee and planned her strategy. There were so many details to review. She must call everyone to make sure that their respective chores were all done. But by 9 o'clock, when she thought it was safe to start calling, the sun had come out, the sky had cleared and according to the weather forecast, it was going to be a nice day after all.

At 1:30, on that bright Saturday afternoon, the bells of St. Andrew's Church began ringing and the wedding guests assembled. At two minutes after two, the strains of Jeremiah Clarke's Trumpet Voluntaire reverberated throughout the traditional building with its rich stained glass windows and impressive arched wooden ceiling. Jimmy came down the aisle flanked by his best man, Roscoe, both wearing white tuxedos with grey lapels and grey, pin-striped tuxedo trousers. Each had a white rose tucked into his lapel buttonhole and Roscoe was carefully carrying the rings in a bright blue box. This had been Claire's idea so that if he happened to drop them before the critical moment they'd be easy to find.

Many eyes were on Jimmy, studying the expression on his face and wondering what he was feeling right then after so many stressful happenings, beginning with his first wife's death. But Claire's eyes were on Roscoe, who was looking proud and serious and was obviously thrilled with the role he'd been asked to play.

Claire's twelve-year-old daughter, Jessie, came down the aisle next, wheeled slowly with one hand by her father, Dan, while with the other he helped her to sprinkle the rose petals from a basket on her wheelchair tray. About halfway down the aisle, Jessie's hand gave out and she began to cry. Dan placed it gently on her tray and grabbed the basket of rose petals before she managed to knock it off. Then he quickly and clumsily pushed the wheelchair the rest of the way down the aisle with his hip while unceremoniously tossing clumps of petals left and right with his other hand, when he wasn't using it to straighten out the chair. With a look of relief, he sank into the front row seat assigned to him and parked Jessie beside him in front of her seat.

Despite her disappointment, Claire, waiting at the back of the aisle, could not resist grinning at the irony of it all. It wasn't the romantic beginning to this ceremony they'd all envisioned but that was the way life was with Jessie—and if anybody didn't like it, too bad! Jessie had more right that most to be part of this ceremony because if it hadn't been for her, Jimmy might be in jail right now for the murder of his first wife or at the very least, living under a cloud of suspicion for life!

Next down the aisle came Claire pushing Mavis, the maid of honor. Janice, a friend of Claire's from her high school days, had patiently cut and styled Mavis' hair that morning, despite her sometimes strenuous objections, and it hung softly around her face with romantic little wisps. On the side of her hair was a simple garland of three white roses. The stylist had even touched up Mavis' eyes and lips with make-up and she truly looked beautiful. Claire also looked lovely in her matching cream gown with a smaller cluster of white roses encircling her wrist.

Claire placed Mavis' chair beside the empty spot awaiting the bride and then took her place on the aisle in the front row. Jimmy turned to his sister Mavis with an awed look and tears in his eyes, appearing to recognize, perhaps for the first time, what an attractive woman she was. Claire knew what he was thinking. He was berating himself for the years she'd lived away from the world where nobody ever saw her like the people here were seeing her today.

There was a momentary hush and then Tia appeared with her father at the back of the church. He was dressed in his good navy suit, freshly cleaned and pressed for the occasion but noticeably shiny with its years of wear and looking slightly on the small side. All Gus' cajoling had not moved him to consider either a new suit or a rented tuxedo and she'd finally given up on that particular battle with as much good grace as was possible for her. Still, she winced slightly when she saw him, noting his home cleaned and pressed slightly off-white and un-crisp white shirt and the scuff marks on his best black shoes that all their vigorous polishing had not managed to quite cover. *Oh, well*, she thought resignedly. *Something always has to go wrong or be slightly off at a wedding. If this is the worst of it then I guess we're lucky.*

Gus need not have worried so much about Alberto's appearance because all eyes were on Tia, not her father. She moved gracefully down the aisle in time to the music, carrying a modest bouquet of white roses and baby's breath, and when she reached Jimmy's side, their eyes locked. Claire moved to take Tia's flowers from her unresisting hand and laid them gently on Mavis' wheelchair tray, discreetly placing Mavis' right hand beneath the tray in the process so she wouldn't knock the flowers off. Then Claire retreated to her aisle seat.

The priest cleared his throat to get the couple's attention and began the beautiful age-old ceremony. "Dearly beloved, we are gathered here today to join together this man and this woman in the holy bonds of matrimony," and he continued on from there. Claire had suggested a couple of tweaks to the traditional ceremony in the interests of feminist correctness, but Tia had not been interested. Nor had she or Jimmy expressed any desire to write their own vows.

"We just want to get it over with," Jimmy had growled.

"As simply and discretely as possible," Tia had added. "Too much of a show is going to look ridiculous considering we've already been living together for six months, and we were both married previously, and I have a nine year old son. Our goals here are to make it clear to anybody who cares that we are now in God's good graces and that we're fully committed to each other for life."

"And to have a damned good party," Jimmy added, "after everything that's happened in the last year!"

Finally, the priest asked for the rings. This was Roscoe's big moment and with shaking fingers he managed to open the box and hand Tia's ring to Jimmy. Claire had taken care to label the box inside with their names so Roscoe wouldn't get confused. Then he handed Jimmy's ring to Tia and stepped back into his place as they'd rehearsed. He did look puzzled by the box, obviously wondering what to do with it, and finally he leaned over and placed it gently on the altar.

The ceremony was over and Father Giacomo informed Jimmy that he could kiss the bride. They took their time with this and then Tia turned towards the audience waiting for Father Giacomo to introduce Jimmy and her as man and wife and for the clapping to begin—but it did not happen.

Instead, Jimmy handed a paper to the priest and took a step away from Tia. Claire rose and guided the surprised Tia back to the seat next to her in the front row that Mario had been occupying. Meanwhile, Jimmy had beckoned Mario to join him.

The priest glanced at the paper, nodded his head and smiled slightly. Then he cleared his throat and began to speak. "As you know, the marriage vows you have just heard are a holy covenant, a public commitment to God before all of you. They do not, in themselves have any legal standing. The legal commitment follows later with the witnessed signing of a legal declaration of marriage by both parties.

But before that signing takes place, we are now going to have a second exchange of vows between two *different* parties. This ceremony also has no legal standing in itself but the associated legalities are underway and I understand that just this morning the last of the legal impediments to them has been removed."

Tia's eyes widened when she heard this and she looked towards Jimmy with surprise. Meanwhile, the audience was listening raptly, waiting for what would happen next.

"Jimmy" Father Giacomo intoned, "do you wish to claim this boy as your son and to care for him and provide for him in all the ways that a loving father looks after a son?"

"I do and I will," Jimmy said, his eyes glistening.

"Mario, are you prepared to accept this man, Jimmy, as your father and to seek guidance from him and to follow his rules as a loving son does to his father?"

"I do and I will." Mario looked shyly at Jimmy and could not manage to keep a small grin off his face despite the solemnity of the occasion.

Father Giacomo then placed one hand on each of their heads and said, "I now bless this new union of father and son that has been publicly declared before me and all of you," gesturing towards the audience, "and which will soon be a legal reality as well."

After a moment of silence, he asked Tia, looking stunned and teary-eyed, to come back to the altar. Claire moved Mavis' chair to one side and Roscoe took a step away on the other side at a signal from the usher. Tia and Jimmy, with Mario between them and all three holding hands turned around to face their friends and family. Father Giacomo then said to the assembly, "I present to you the Elves family—Mr. and Mrs. Jimmy Elves and their son, Mario, soon to be legally known as Mario Elves."

The audience was stunned and obviously touched by this additional ceremony but before anyone could respond Bill started chanting in a loud voice, "Elves, Elves, Elves! Mae-Mae-Elves! Mae-Mae Elves! Not Mario Elves. Mae-Mae…." but Tom had risen from his seat on the other side of Bill and led Bill quickly and quietly out the side door.

After a brief hesitation to get past this latest bit of drama, the crowd cheered and Mario looked at them in awe, somewhat overwhelmed by their obvious pleasure at what they had witnessed. But he noticed that standing just inside the church at the very back was a tall, somewhat heavy set man with a face that seemed creased and old-looking even though he was obviously still quite young. He was not clapping but instead was just standing there, looking sadly at Mario. Mario looked questioningly at his mother and he felt her hand tense and heard the slight catch of her breath. It seemed to him that she was expecting something to happen then but nothing did. Instead, the man turned and walked quickly out of the church just as the first notes of Henry Purcell's 'Trumpet Tune in D' began, to usher the newly minted Elves family out.

Chapter 43: Too Good to Last

The wedding guests reconvened that evening for the dinner and dance at the hall. The buffet was a great success with all the beef and mashed potatoes anyone could want, two types of delicious lasagna and a rich variety of salads. Many of the side dishes had been contributed by Italian friends and relatives, who'd been part of Tia's life since childhood. There was even a large platter of Risotto con Porcini provided by Marisa's friend, Concetta. She declared to all who would listen that she'd smuggled the seeds out of Italy and into Canada many years ago and since then had always grown these most delicious of Italian mushrooms in the shady patches of her background which mimicked the conditions of the northern Italian forests where they grew in the wild.

Hilda's and Marion's Pineapple Charlotte was a great success, as was the huge pan of Tiramisu Marisa had made, laced with espresso and two types of Italian liqueur she wouldn't identify, claiming it was her own special recipe. At Claire's insistence, she had grudgingly flanked it with a note warning that it contained alcohol, which it did in generous amounts. This had caused a temporary resurgence of her all but forgotten early feelings of animosity towards "the English," meaning native-born Canadians. "What difference did it make if children ingested a little alcohol in the cake?" she had asked. They did so all the time in Italy and it hadn't destroyed them!

After the buffet was over, the food was cleared away, the big tables stacked in one corner and the chairs pushed back to make room for the dancing. Among the wedding guests were Tia's Zio Luigi and her cugino, Vinni. Vinni was the cousin who'd loaned her the lock picks that had come in so handy during a couple of Tia's earlier escapades.

Together, Luigi and Vinni organized everyone into a group Tarantella dance, instructing as they went along. This proved to be a great icebreaker and after that, the majority of the guests were happy to dance away without regard to perfect form to a variety of Italian polkas, waltzes and quick steps.

Throughout the evening, there were various speeches including a heartfelt toast to the bride from Claire who described what Tia's friendship had meant to her and shared a little of Tia's story, as she understood it, as well as a few tidbits from some of their past adventures together. Rifts and wounds had healed enough so that she was able to include the tale of the Mérrida fiasco that brought alternate *oohs* at their bravery and laughs at their antics. Jimmy just smiled grimly but said nothing. Later though, when he walked by Claire, he spontaneously put his arm around her and she finally felt forgiven.

Mavis and Bill returned to their home at nine with Tom and a new female assistant, Emily, escorting them. Roscoe, however, was hugely enjoying himself. While Bill had been content to just stand in front of one of the speakers swaying back and forth to the beat of the music and Mavis had placed her hands on her ears signaling that she needed to be kept far away from them, Roscoe had been out on the dance floor moving with enthusiasm if not finesse. Claire watched him happily as he later travelled the perimeter of the room, introducing himself to people he didn't know and stopping for a chat with those he'd met previously. He seemed to her to be more like his old self than he had been in a long time.

At 10 o'clock, as pre-arranged, Tia and Jimmy left to spend their wedding night and the remainder of the weekend in a honeymoon suite at Fantasyland Hotel. They would return home Monday afternoon. Tia had refused to take a regular honeymoon at this point because of Roscoe's increasingly dangerous situation. She'd also thought it a waste of money to stay in a fancy hotel. However, her friends were able to short circuit her objections by presenting a complete honeymoon package to the couple as a group-wedding gift. It included not only the beautiful room for two nights but meals and twin massages. And since Claire informed Tia that it was non-refundable, there was not much Tia could do but graciously accept it. Jimmy had grinned happily when they received the reservation for the honeymoon package. He was slowly learning to appreciate Claire's conniving mind.

The guests began gradually leaving after the wedding couple's departure. Tia's parents left first with an exhausted Mario in tow. They were staying at his home with him for the weekend. Gus and Amanda left shortly after and took Marion with them. They had invited her to stay over at their house so they could have a nice rehash in the morning about the wedding events. Also, Hilda wanted to stay behind and help with the cleaning-up and therefore could not drive her home. Several friends of Tia stayed also to help—and Roscoe also insisted on staying.

"I hep!" he said to the others. "*I* know how. Claih show me. I do it lots uh time a the Picafish Sop." This was Roscoe's unique way of referring to 'The Piccadilly Fish and Chip Shoppe'.

Claire realized at that moment how much she genuinely liked Roscoe as a *person,* not just a client. She remembered how attentive he'd been and how carefully he'd tried to copy her when she showed him how to sweep the floor at the café without raising dust and how to clean the bathrooms. "Dan and I can drive him home later," she told Tom, who'd come back after getting Mavis and Bill into their beds to be with Roscoe and to help out.

Soon, everyone was gone but Claire, Dan and Roscoe. Roscoe swept slowly and methodically across the floor, regularly filling and emptying the dustpan as he went. Dan had gathered up all the bottles and taken them to the recycle bin outside and Claire had polished the kitchen sinks and counters to perfection but still Roscoe was sweeping. Dan looked at Claire impatiently. "We really should get home and get the babysitter home. I could have swept the floor ten times by now."

"I know but that's not the point," Claire replied. Can't you see how proud he is—and how important it is for him to help me? I can't take that away from him and finishing the job for him would just trivialize his efforts. If you want to have a real relationship with Roscoe—and he's well *worth* having a real relationship with—then you have to learn patience, which is actually not such a bad thing in this crazy world. And, by the way, I already fixed up the spare bed for Ella and told her just to go to sleep when she was tired but to leave her door open so she could hear Jessie if she wakes up. I knew we were going to be late."

Shortly after midnight, they finally left the building and the only task remaining was to make sure the door was securely locked. There were two locks and one was a bit tricky. Dan was grateful that the outside security light remained on as he struggled to make sure both locks were done correctly. Claire and Roscoe stood at the bottom of the steps patiently waiting for him.

A dark car cruised slowly down the deserted street in front of them and suddenly a shot rang out hitting Roscoe's left arm! The hall door was locked at this point and Dan had been heading down the steps. They had no choice but to race to the relative safety of the car. They were too vulnerable standing there. Dan grabbed Roscoe by his uninjured arm and the three of them ran, expecting more bullets at any second but the dark car had raced away after firing that single shot.

Dan unlocked the car doors with the remote and Claire raced to get in the back seat on the other side so she could help Roscoe. But Roscoe seemed frozen with fear at this point and was not responding to Dan's urging to get in the car. Dan had to resort to physically pushing him in while Claire pulled, all the time trying to avoid Roscoe's injured arm and waiting for a second bullet to come their way. Finally, Roscoe was in and Dan was able to close the door. He jumped into the driver's seat, locked the doors from the front control and raced away.

When they reached the first corner, Claire asked him to turn and stop the car. "I have to check his arm and call the police and maybe the ambulance!" Roscoe was shaking violently at this point and it was clear that he was going into shock.

"But we're just five minutes from his house. Wouldn't it be better to go there so we can look after him properly?"

"I don't know!" Claire groaned. "He's bleeding so much. Roscoe, Roscoe, talk to me!" But Roscoe had slumped against the corner of the seat with his eyes closed and his teeth chattering loudly. Just then there was a loud pounding at the window and Claire screamed. Dan jumped violently, fearing the worst. But when he looked out he saw the concern on the man's face and rolled down the window.

"I live across from the hall," he said without preamble, "and I saw what happened. My wife's calling the police and an ambulance and they should be here soon. She said to give you this blanket. How is he?" he asked, peering at Roscoe in the back seat.

"Not good," Claire sobbed. "He's in shock and I don't know how badly he's hurt. There's a lot of blood and he won't let me touch his arm." She wrapped the blanket gently around Roscoe and thanked the man.

Just then they heard sirens and the man raced back to the corner waving frantically at the ambulance. It followed his directions and pulled to a stop beside them seconds later. A patrol car followed almost immediately, guided by the ambulance siren.

One of the paramedics opened the back door on Roscoe's side of the car and spoke to him. "Hello, sir. My name is Fred and I'm a paramedic. I'm here to help you. How badly are you hurt, sir?" Roscoe just stared at him dully. The man pulled out a huge pair of scissors so he could cut Roscoe's sleeve off and Roscoe screamed.

Claire reached across Roscoe and pushed the man away angrily. "Don't touch him and put those scissors away. He's frightened of them! I'll come around and help you get him out."

Claire went around to Roscoe's door, pushing Fred further back, away from Roscoe's view. Dan slid into the back seat preparatory to pushing Roscoe out if he had to. "Roscoe, the man was not going to hurt you," Claire said. "He only needed the scissors to cut your sleeve off so he could fix your arm."

"No-o-o!" Roscoe wailed. "He wec the jacka and i-s not mine. Jimmy will be mad. We have to give it back. Not *wec* it!"

In a sudden flash, Claire understood what was going through his mind and felt a new surge of admiration for him. Even bleeding and in pain, he was thinking of his responsibility to others. She turned to the paramedic who'd been standing there patiently. "As difficult as it is, we're going to have to figure a way to get his jacket and shirt off without ripping them. It's a rental suit and he's very concerned about not damaging it and there's no way I'm going to be able to talk him out of that. It's part of his condition," Claire explained wearily.

Fred nodded his head in understanding and Claire explained to Roscoe that they were going to try to get his clothes off without ripping them but he'd have to get out of the car so they could do that and then attend to his arm. He agreed, Dan pushed and they finally got him out but Roscoe was very weak by this time and looked like he was going to fall. Claire tugged and pulled while Roscoe moaned and Fred and Dan struggled to keep him upright. Finally, the jacket came off and Claire unbuttoned the shirt. It was soaked through with blood and blood was still oozing out of his arm and the shirt was stuck tight to it. Fred shook his head.

"We can't save the shirt, Roscoe," Claire said gently, "but we can buy the people a new one. Shirts don't cost too much. Roscoe was sagging so much at this point that the decision was made for him and Fred and his partner, Andrea, lowered him onto the stretcher and lifted it into the ambulance. "We're taking him to the Grey Nuns Hospital. You can follow us."

Claire looked at Dan. "I'll go with you," she said. My husband has to go home and check on our daughter. "Okay, Dan?" she said, turning to him. But just then a car wheeled up and Inspector McCoy got out.

"Here!" he said harshly to Claire. "You can't leave. I need to talk to you!" Dan had explained to the officers in the patrol car what had happened when they first arrived and when they had radioed in Roscoe's name McCoy was automatically notified.

"I'm going with Roscoe. He needs me. Dan can tell you everything."

She hopped in the back, the door was closed and the ambulance took off. By this time, Andrea had managed to cut Roscoe's shirt off and he was covered with a warming blanket. Fred was driving and Andrea swabbed the wound and expertly dressed it. The sudden sharp pain from the antiseptic brought Roscoe out of the stupor he'd been in and he shuddered all over. Andrea quickly inserted an iv needle in his good arm and began a glucose drip to bring him out of the shock.

Claire stroked Roscoe's head and spoke to him in soothing tones. Roscoe tried to talk then. "Why? W-h-y? Why that man hurt me? *I* no tell. *I* no tell." He rocked back and forth on the stretcher as he suddenly realized the full impact of what had happened to him and Claire and Andrea had to hold him down to keep him from disconnecting the iv.

Claire, herself, was feeling nauseated and shaky at this point, overcome by warring feelings of sadness and anger. *Why, indeed?* she asked herself. Roscoe had just been showing the first signs of recovery. He'd been happy tonight, for the first time in a long time. Happy and proud. And now *this!*

After Claire and Roscoe left in the ambulance, Inspector McCoy and the officers took Dan back to the hall so he could explain exactly what had happened and where they'd been standing at the time. The officers scrutinized the ground with high-powered flashlights and finally found the bullet casing under the steps. The bullet itself was lying in plain view on the second step. It apparently had passed right through the soft tissue in Roscoe's arm and landed there. The officers also checked for the tire marks of the car that sped away but Dan's own hasty departure had largely obscured them. They took copious pictures from all angles and then gave the memory card, the bullet and the casing to Inspector McCoy, promised they would email him a copy of their notes the next day and they left. They were patrol cops, not a forensic team, and could not help any further. McCoy went over the incident with Dan once more and then let him go.

At the hospital Roscoe's arm was x-rayed just to make sure the bone was okay. He was given a strong sedative and left to sleep as best he could in a bed in the emergency ward overnight. Claire curled up on a mattress beside him and thought ruefully that she should have followed Dan's initial idea and gone directly to the house.

When Roscoe awoke the next day, he was given a strong pain killer which left him groggy and wanting to sleep more. His arm was checked and redressed and by 11 o'clock he had been signed out and Daisuke came to pick them up. Claire had called him that morning to tell him what had happened but asked him not to say anything to Roscoe's parents until they had him back at the house. She had also phoned Tom and Emily and warned them not to talk to anybody else about the incident. Above all, she did not want Tia and Jimmy to know and have their pathetically short, two-day honeymoon ruined for them.

When Claire got home, she looked helplessly at Roscoe's bloodstained jacket. Tia would know what to do but she could not ask her right now. Finally, she put it in a tub of cold water along with the pants which were now much the worse for wear, reasoning that she could not take them to the cleaners in that condition.

Chapter 44: Another Dead End

Tia and Jimmy arrived home at 1:30 on Monday afternoon looking happy and relaxed and Claire, Gus and Amanda were there to meet them.

"It was better than I thought it would be at the hotel––almost worth the money it cost you," Tia acknowledged. "It's kind of nice to be treated like a queen once in a while!"

"And the food was great—among other things!" Jimmy grinned. Tia blushed.

For half an hour, they talked on about the hotel amenities and how much fun they had had in the wave pool. "I tried every single one of the slides and then we grabbed some inner tubes that people had discarded and went out in the deep end where the waves were really strong. I wish they had had pools like that when *I* was a kid!" Jimmy exclaimed.

Claire thought he was still sounding like a kid but it was good to hear coming from this man who'd been alternately somber and sour for much of the time she'd known him. She encouraged them to continue talking, describing everything and reliving the experience as much as they wished to. Then the others chimed in, rehashing the wedding and the dance, the best parts of it, the few screw-ups, and odd comments they'd heard from the guests. It was generally agreed that the whole thing had been a great success, even better than they could have hoped for.

When the wedding conversation finally died down and Gus and Amanda were showing signs of leaving,

Claire said, "I have something I have to tell you"—and she told them what had happened to Roscoe.

Tia and Jimmy were completely shocked and Tia's first response was one of anger. "Why didn't you *call* me?" she asked huffily.

"Why do you think, Tia? What exactly could you have done—except ruin the little bit of time you had for your honeymoon?"

"Thanks!" Jimmy said grimly. "You were right, Claire. It wouldn't have helped Roscoe and it certainly would have wrecked things for us."

"But what about us, then? Why didn't you tell *us*?" Gus demanded to know.

Claire took a moment so she could phrase her response as diplomatically as possible. "I thought the fewer people who knew the better. That way it had less chance of getting back to Jimmy and Tia. I didn't even tell Roscoe's parents until after we brought him back from the hospital the next day. Do you really think there's any point in upsetting people unnecessarily when there's nothing they can do to help?"

"What I *think* is we have to find this killer before he finally succeeds in finishing Roscoe off!" Tia interjected. "And I'm not prepared to sit around any longer waiting for the answer to fall into our lap! I want to take action."

"What action?" Jimmy asked. "You and Claire have done everything you can do. As I see it, there are no leads left to follow up."

"*I* think we've been side-tracked," Tia said. "Don't you agree, Claire?"

"Yes, I do. We've become fixated on this elusive bicycle guy—when the only solid lead we *really* have is the bottle you found in the cafe and the matching bottles in that Mérrida factory."

"There was nothing in their house," Tia mused. "The answer has to be in that café. I have to have *missed* something."

"Well, you're not going back there after this!" Jimmy blustered.

"I have to!" Tia said stubbornly.

"I kind of agree with Jimmy on this. That bullet could have hit any of us. I think whoever is targeting Roscoe is getting desperate."

"What is Inspector McCoy doing to find him, Claire?"

"He sent detectives out to talk to all the neighbors and one of them said he saw a dark car sitting across the street from the hall when they looked out the window a couple of times during the evening. Another person said she saw a man peeping in the hall windows late that evening but she couldn't see his face. He could have easily seen that Roscoe was still there."

"Fine. But what's he going to do now? And where is Sergeant Crombie? What's *he* saying?"

"McCoy was alone the night it happened. He said Sergeant Crombie and his wife were in Calgary visiting their son. His son's wife just had a baby boy, their first grand-child."

"So *he*'s out of the loop—and McCoy is at a dead end again, just like us!"

Chapter 45: Tia Takes a Chance

There was more bad news still to come for Tia and Jimmy that day. At 3:30 that afternoon Jimmy received a phone call from his aunt. Uncle Ted, his mother's brother, had had a heart attack and was not expected to live. They had no children and Aunt Louise asked him if he could come. Tia agreed that he should go and spend the night and offer what support he could to his aunt and visit his uncle—possibly for the last time.

As it happened, Mario had a sleepover with one of his friends that Monday night since they had a holiday from school the next day, a professional development day. Tia was left all alone and by seven o'clock, she was feeling a bit sorry for herself. She contemplated opening a bottle of wine and watching TV, but then she mentally chided herself. Claire was getting her into bad habits—turning to drink whenever something good happened or something bad happened. She made a cup of tea instead and tried to read the mystery book Claire had loaned her, but she couldn't get into it. Tia wasn't as much of a reader as Claire was, always preferring to keep busy doing something instead.

She put the book down with a sigh and contemplated turning the TV on—but then she had an idea. Both Jimmy and Claire had urged her not to return to the Shoppe, as they had taken to calling it, and in any case the Wus were not expecting her tonight because of her honeymoon. But Lan had always made it clear she did not care what night Tia came as long as she did the job. Strangely for such a genial guy, Chen was a bit more formal, wanting to know what days she was coming and even what time. He clearly liked order and predictability. Tia could respect that. She was like that herself.

If she went tonight, Tia reasoned, she would not have to argue with Jimmy about it and since she fully intended to keep going one way or another she could not see the harm in it. Maybe that was Claire's "bad influence" again, as Jimmy had said about some of her other rebellious ideas. "Whatever," Tia mumbled, and got up to get ready to leave. She just knew there must be something she hadn't found despite all the times she'd been there—and Tia had an idea where she needed to look.

Once she got into the café, Tia didn't feel the usual energy and interest in her cleaning efforts. She cleaned quickly and methodically but perhaps not quite as meticulously as she usually did. She hurried along, not remaining in the usual rhythm she'd established and feeling resentful every time she came across an unexpected extra cleaning task. "People are such slobs!" she muttered to herself.

Finally, she felt she'd done all that could be expected to do for one evening. The bathrooms were clean, the floors washed and the kitchen counters and stovetop wiped off. She chose to ignore the film of grease gathering on the overhead vent that would only be back the next time she came, no matter what she did tonight.

Tia turned her attention to the office. It was always locked when she arrived in the evening. A few times, she'd come earlier while the Wus were still there and then she'd been able to vacuum and dust and clean the light fixtures, which badly needed it. But Lan told her it was not necessary to clean the office regularly as nobody used it but them. "Odd notion of clean" Tia had thought, "but it's *their* office."

Tia did not plan to clean it tonight either but she parked the vacuum outside the door so that in the unlikely event that one of the Wus came in, she could explain that she'd found the door unlocked and was taking the opportunity to do some cleaning there. "Once in a while every room needed to be cleaned no matter how lightly it has been used." This was the line she rehearsed to herself before tackling the door. It was locked and she used Vinni's lock picks to get it open. She managed this in about three minutes, being quite practiced at this point. Vinni had given up asking for the picks back since she seemed to have more use for them than he did.

Tia put on some disposable gloves so she wouldn't leave marks on the furniture and began her task. She quickly and methodically went through the desk and drawers looking for any reference to the word, 'Mérrida'. Nothing! She felt for a hidden shelf under the sofa and removed the chair and sofa cushions. Nothing! Yet something told her she was right. She went back to the desk and felt at the back of the shallow middle drawer, looking for a hidden compartment. Nothing. Then she felt under the drawer. Maybe there was a key. No key—but she did feel a kind of knob on the drawer glide. She pushed on it and heard a click.

Startled, she looked towards the door, which she'd left ajar, to see if anybody was there, but the hall was empty. She turned to the bookshelf behind the desk. She'd been through the few books and magazines there, mostly restaurant guides and books on how to run a small business. She had found nothing. Now she reached out to examine the shelves themselves, two three-foot wide and five and a half feet tall walnut stained shelves. Starting with the first one, she felt up and down all the shelves but found nothing. But when her hand accidentally brushed the second shelf in the process it seemed to move slightly. She pushed harder and the whole shelf moved in, revealing a small, hidden room behind it. Tia stared at it in amazement. What do you know? She'd been *right!* There *was* something to discover.

It was dark in the little room but there was enough light from the office to show a light switch just inside the door. When she turned it on, Tia realized with a thrill of fear that she'd found what she was looking for. Along one wall to the left of the door was a high counter with a very fancy scale on it. All along the back wall was a bank of shallow cupboards and drawers. When Tia opened a cupboard door, she found a bin full of small bags of white powder and she was pretty sure they weren't icing sugar. Tia grabbed her phone and called Claire. This was too good to wait.

"Hi, Claire, I'm at the shoppe and…."

"What? You promised not to go there! Please leave right now or I'm going to call Jimmy!"

"Jimmy's not home and let me tell you…."

"Tell her what?" came a voice from the office door.

Tia looked in shock at the two men standing there. One of them was holding a gun and the other one was Wu Chen. But this was a different Wu Chen than she'd ever seen before. There was no genial smile on his face this time. Meanwhile, Claire was asking her what was happening and Tia discreetly pushed the speaker button and nudged the phone to the back of the counter near the door without ending the call. Then she walked into the office leaving the door behind her open.

"I'm sorry, Chen. I was dusting the desk and dust often collects underneath desks in the drawer glides. When I dusted there, I hit a little button and heard a noise. I turned around quickly and my elbow hit this shelf here and then it started to move. I was about to tell my friend about this cute little room when you came in." It sounded weak to her ears but it was the best she could do. She was thanking God fervently for her upbringing that had caused her to automatically close the door where the white powder was stored. She could claim she'd never opened it and had never seen anything unusual.

But Chen wasn't buying it and his friend even less so. "How did you get in here?" he asked. "Don't you keep the door locked, Chen?"

"Yes, normally. I can't actually remember if I locked it today when I left. I assumed I had."

"It wasn't locked," Tia said smoothly. "I finished early tonight and I tried the door just in case. I thought I would do a little cleaning in here while I had the chance."

"Then why is the vacuum cleaner still outside?" the strange man asked. Chen continued to say nothing.

"I always dust first. Otherwise, you just end up doing twice the work," Tia said, and hoped fervently that they wouldn't check out the dust cloth she had placed strategically on top of the desk because it was still completely clean. But the unknown man did.

"She's lying. She knows. You should never have had her working here at night alone anyway," the man snarled at Chen.

"Lan arranged it. What was I supposed to say to her?"

"Well, it's done now. We'll have to get rid of her."

"You said no more...."

"Shut up!"

"Not *here!"* You'll get blood all over!"

"No. Let's get her into the car. We'll take her out in the bush and do it there. Easier to dump the body."

The man grabbed Tia roughly by the arm and started hauling her towards the building door. She fought him as best she could but he was too strong for her. All she could manage was to flick her wallet out of the little purse she still had slung over her neck when they reached the road. Maybe whoever came would see it there on the ground and figure out that she'd been taken. Surely Claire would have called the police by now.

Chapter 46: Claire Acts

Claire listened in horror to the snatches of conversation she managed to overhear from Tia's phone. Then she hear a muffled, scuffling sound and knew she had to act. She screamed for Dan. When he appeared, she yelled at him hysterically. "Call the police and tell them to go to the café! The address is on the fridge." Claire had added the fridge decal she'd received from the Shoppe on her first visit there to her growing collection on the fridge door. "And tell them it's McCoy's case. Tia has been attacked and they're taking her away to kill her!"

Dan stared at her stunned, but Claire was busy grabbing her keys and her purse and hurtling out the door. She turned one last time as she left. "Do it *now!*" she begged.

Dan ran after her instead, but by this time she was in her car, fortunately still parked in the driveway. Claire locked the doors, gunned the motor and started backing out. Dan ran beside the car banging on the door.

"No, no, Claire! Don't go! It's too *dangerous!"* he begged. But she was gone and he couldn't go after her because he was now home alone with Jessie. He grabbed a phone and called 911.

Claire raced to the café as fast as she could drive, almost hoping that a cruising patrol car would see her and give chaise. At least that way she'd have backup because she knew how dangerous this was going to be. She hadn't even told Dan about the gun. He must have a gun or Chen wouldn't have been talking about getting blood all over!

She turned the last corner just in time to see the two men pushing Tia into the back seat of a car. Then they jumped in the front and took off fast. Claire did not even slow down. She speeded up instead, as fast as she dared. If they got away, the police would never catch them in time to save Tia!

The abductors were forced to stop at a red light because of traffic crossing in front of them and Claire made a split second choice. She did not brake at all but angled slightly to the side of them and drove their car head on into a convenient light pole. The crash buckled the pole and inflated both front air bags in their vehicle, effectively pinning the men in their seats. Claire caught a fleeting glimpse of Tia bouncing forward and then back before Claire's own air bag inflated and she could see nothing more and was herself pinned down. Her last thought before she lost consciousness was that if Tia had a concussion or a sprained neck it was *still* better than being dead!

When Claire awoke, it was to hear a severe grinding sound that immediately gave her a violent headache—or maybe she already had a headache and this was making it worse! Dimly, she realized what was happening. An emergency crew was working to get her door open. Her air bag was now deflated and she could see that the whole frame of her car was badly twisted. That must be why they were having so much trouble getting her door open.

Finally, the door gave way with a particularly horrible screeching sound and two paramedics moved in to check her over before gently lifting her onto a body board and then transferring her to a waiting ambulance. "Tia!" she gasped. "Look after Tia!" and she promptly passed out again.

Chapter 47: Two Scared Men

Claire awoke in hospital many hours later, not because she'd been so badly hurt, although she did have a mild concussion from the impact. However, she'd been so agitated when the paramedics brought her in, asking over and over about Tia's state and demanding to know if they'd caught the murderers that the on-call doctor assumed she was hallucinating. He'd ordered a strong sedative for her that knocked her out and a CT scan to find out if there was any bleed in the brain. The CT scan came back negative.

When Claire did awake it was to find two men standing over her—Dan and Inspector McCoy. They both looked relieved but neither of them looked happy.

"Did you get them? Did you find their stash?" she croaked in McCoy's direction.

Before he could even answer, she turned to Dan. "Tia! Is Tia okay?"

"I'm fine," came a voice from the door. Tia walked in, limping slightly. She knelt beside Claire's bed and put her arms around her gently. "You could have been killed!" she sobbed.

"You *would* have been killed. I didn't know what else to *do!"*

The on-call doctor came in at this point to check Claire and all conversation had to stop. He closed the curtains around her bed and proceeded to do a thorough exam, checking first for double vision, ringing in the ears, head-ache, stiff neck and then moving on down to see if there were any unusually sore spots, difficult to tell since everything was a little bit sore. Finally, he declared that she was in good enough shape to be discharged and he would sign the papers. She could leave when she was ready, but needed to stop by the desk first and wait to be wheeled out.

After dressing and sitting down with Inspector McCoy to provide her preliminary statement, Claire and Dan were finally free to leave. It was only Thursday, less than a week since Tia and Jimmy had been married, and Claire could not believe how much had happened.

Chapter 48: It Begins to Make Sense

Saturday evening, two days later, a very different celebration took place than the wedding the Saturday before. Roscoe, his parents, Marion, Hilda, Claire, Dan, Gus, and Amanda met at the home of Tia and Jimmy to rehash all that had happened and clear up any loose ends so they could put the story behind them. Tia had also invited Inspector McCoy and surprisingly he came.

"He's probably feeling guilty because once again we did most of the work and took all the risks but he gets the credit for busting an international drug operation," Claire had told Tia sourly, when she heard he was planning to come. "But, at least, Inspector Romero will get credit for *his* part in the investigation. It was a big drug-bust and he told me he's up for promotion to District Inspector."

Tia began, telling her story up to the time she had been abducted and how Claire had 'rescued' her "although she could have just as easily killed me in the process," Tia added.

"It was kill or cure," Claire muttered.

Tia laughed. "Of *course* you would have yet another cliché to describe even *this* situation."

Inspector McCoy then weighed in. "We arrested the men at the scene. Dan had called so I knew what was happening. They weren't badly hurt but your insurance company will still have to pay out to cover the damages," he said, turning to Claire. "The law doesn't make special allowances for citizen's arrests." Claire winced but then caught the half grin on his face. Was there actually a tiny glimmer of respect in his eyes for what she'd done? That would almost make the inevitably higher insurance premiums worthwhile.

Inspector McCoy continued with the story. "We went back to the Shoppe after that and found the drugs in bags just like Tia said when we got her out of that car. Analysis has proved them to be high quality cocaine. They were in hermetically sealed bags with a special stamp over the seam to prevent them from being tampered with by the dealers.

By the way, the man arrested with Wu Chen turned out to be his older brother, Wu Heng and the two young men living with Chen and Lan are Wu Heng's sons."

"So that's why she told me that the one I saw was a nephew—but I'm sure she said *her* nephew!"

"In our language we don't make a distinction and I bet it's the same in Mandarin. The two languages are closely related," Roscoe's mother, Yuna, said.

"Anyway," McCoy went on, "because of the earlier bicycle incident with Roscoe, we brought both boys in for questioning. It turns out they have similar bikes, but the older one, Wu Denin, known to his friends as Nick Wu, couldn't account for his actions at the time of the incident and came across as uncooperative and furtive. Your grandson, Gerald, provided us with the names of a couple of the students at the college who had drug dealings with him," McCoy said, turning to Yuna.

"Apparently," McCoy went on, oblivious to Yuna's scowl at her older grandson, "he'd taken it upon himself to find some cocaine users there and see if he could track down their source. They told him that Wu Denin used to hang around in the quad, the open space between the two college buildings, between 3 and 3:30 most afternoons and that's when Gerald could meet up with him if he wanted to buy drugs. Wu Denin never came on Wednesdays, though. He told a couple of the students he sold to that he had to supply his downtown dealer on Wednesdays. Apparently, he kind of bragged about it. Two of the other students my detectives talked to confirmed that—although they stressed that they, themselves, were not users."

Everyone laughed when McCoy said this. "The rest of the story we got from Wu Denin, himself," McCoy went on. "He likes to come across as the tough guy but it did not take much to break him under questioning."

McCoy continued with the story. "Wu Denin's Wednesday routine was to load his bike on the LRT well before rush hour while it was still allowed on and then get off at Corona Station where he met his contact and supplied him with cocaine for distributing to his users at St. Joseph's High School and a couple of other big centers. Wu Heng trusted him to do this and Wu Denin considered it a great honor.

Anyway, when he got off the LRT at Corona Station that day he, just by fluke, saw Roscoe and Claire coming towards the station steps and he rolled his bike back down the sidewalk a bit and waited for his chance. When he figured Roscoe was positioned just right he drove into him."

"We should sue him!" Claire growled.

"Well, it's over anyway," McCoy responded. "We've got them locked up now and Roscoe should be safe. And I have to admit that we could not have done it without your help," he said, turning to Tia and Claire.

"I hep, too, Mr. McCoy. I tell you the man!" Roscoe interjected.

"That is true, Roscoe! You came to the police station and identified the man who killed Sam from an identity line-up. That *really* helped us!"

"Mr. Wu's brudder, dat's who," Roscoe said, nodding his head up and down.

"And he's going to be in jail for a very long time and you won't have to worry anymore about him hurting you."

Inspector McCoy left then, returning briefly to his officious ways by warning them that they must not share any of this information with others, explaining that he had only told it to them as a special concession because of all they'd done and all that Roscoe had been through.

"Wow!" Claire said, after he left, "McCoy is really coming along!"

Chapter 49: One Last Surprise

Just then the doorbell rang. Tia went to open it and immediately took a step back. Daisuke was standing there with Yeung Lan.

"I am sorry I am late," he said. "I had to wait for that inspector to leave. May we come in?" he asked politely. "This lady has something to tell you."

Tia motioned them in and they joined her in the living room. There was a collective gasp and Roscoe got up as if to leave. But before that could happen, and before Daisuke could even introduce her, Yeung Lan spoke for herself.

"Roscoe," she said in a soft voice, "I want to apologize for my bad behavior towards you in the café before you left. It is no excuse but I have been under a lot of stress for a long time. I took it out on you and that was wrong."

"Those girls bad," he mumbled, not quite looking at her.

"I know that now. You were right."

Roscoe looked slightly mollified but did not seem to know what to say. Daisuke made the belated introductions then and ended by saying that Yeung Lan had a story to tell them, and he asked her to go ahead.

"When my husband and I left Beijing seven years ago, we took with us the two sons of Wu Heng. His wife, Zhang Chunhua, died when the boys were only six and ten, and Wu Heng did not want them. He allowed us to adopt them. He came to Canada, to Edmonton, and later he helped us to come here. Wu

Gen was twelve by then and Wu Denin was sixteen. Wu Gen fit right into the school situation and did well and has good friends there but Wu Denin did not. He is very smart though and he managed to finish school and went on to college to study business.

"What was he doing at the college all day, then?" Claire asked. The director told Inspector McCoy that Wu Denin had dropped most of his courses and was only still registered in one.

"I never knew what he was doing during the day. He seemed to have money and he talked vaguely of working. Lots of nights he did not even come home and I knew he was spending more and more time with Wu Heng. He idolized him and longed to be accepted by him. He thought Wu Chen was soft and not a very good businessman. If Denin attacked Roscoe on the bike it was to protect Wu Heng from being identified as Sam's killer."

"So-o," Jimmy said slowly. "It was Wu Denin who knocked Roscoe down with his bike. But what about the other incidents—and who was stalking him in the black car…and what about the bike Amanda saw?"

"I talked to him in the jail and he told me a lot of things," Yeung Lan said. "He was driving the car the night of your wedding party when Wu Heng shot Roscoe. And he did admit to riding his bike by Roscoe's house a few times to try to figure out Roscoe's schedule. But the other things and staking out Roscoe's house with the black car was all Wu Heng's doing."

After a pause, Yeung Lan added, "I feel like we let him down somehow, that we should have done more to keep him from Wu Heng's influence but he has been so defiant every time I tried to tell him something these past few years that I guess I just gave up. And then, of course, I did not know how involved in all this Wu Chen was."

"Well, I guess that pretty well answers all our questions," Dan commented. He turned to Tia and Claire and said, "I guess you two can put another notch on your belts—and I sincerely hope that it will be the last one."

"I second that!" Jimmy said, fervently.

But the other members of the group were not willing to let it go at that. Too many bad things had happened not to require further explanation. Tia started. "Yeung Lan, how is it that your English is suddenly so good?"

"I studied hard. I went to night school here many years. But Wu Chen has no ear for languages and he still sounds like he arrived here yesterday. I talk like him in the store so customers will not talk to me and ignore him. I have tried very hard to make our marriage work for the sake of the boys but since we came here he has fallen more and more under the influence of Wu Heng".

"Mr. Wu always nice to me," Roscoe blurted. "Y*ou* not nice to me. Why?"

Yeung Lan looked at Roscoe, started to speak and then stopped. She started again. "Wu and I have not been getting along for some time. He was never much of a businessman but he used to be a nice man. Not anymore. He started relying on Wu Heng to advise him and then he seemed to change. Now, of course, we all know why but I had no idea he was smuggling in cocaine with his brother. I asked him to leave the house a few months before you came because he hardly spoke to us anymore and always seemed to be preoccupied. The only one he bothered with was Wu Denin and they used to go out in the garage together and drink beer and watch the TV he put there. He made a kind of place for himself there."

"A man cave," Claire commented.

"Anyway, I guess I was still angry with him even when we got back together and I took it out on you, Roscoe. I'm sorry."

Gus looked at her shrewdly. "There is more to it than that, isn't there?"

Yeung Lan looked at Roscoe, and Claire tried to interrupt, guessing what was coming, but Gus persisted. "After everything that has happened, I think we have a right to know the whole story. If Wu Chen is the bad one in this story and you are the good one, then why was he always so nice to Roscoe while you were so nasty?"

Like many female narcissists, Gus basically liked men better than women, with whom she felt herself to be in competition. Hence, she was having a hard time wrapping her mind around Wu Chen as the villain and Yeung Lan as just another victim like them. She was still secretly wondering if somehow Yeung Lan had managed to twist the story around and if, at the very least, she'd been involved in this whole scheme, if not, in fact, the mastermind behind it.

Gus' suspicions were quite transparent to Yeung Lan who was highly attuned to reading prejudice and dismissal in the remarks of others. She responded viscerally, without regard for Roscoe or anyone else. "You want the reason. I'll *give* you the reason—actually, *three* reasons. When Claire phoned Wu Chen about the possibility of a work placement for Roscoe he agreed to meet with them but then phoned Wu Heng for advice. To his surprise, Wu Heng thought it was a brilliant idea. He told Wu Chen to hire Roscoe conditionally, on the understanding that Claire would stick around and train him to do the job properly as she said she would."

"An I din do good job, dinn't I, Claih?" Roscoe interjected. He had a confused and worried look on his face and his enunciation was even worse than usual because of his obvious stress."

"Yes, you did, Roscoe," Claire said, supportively. "And you learned very quickly, *too.*" That was all she could say or do. The train had been set in motion and she had a terrible premonition as to where it was going to end up. And when she repeated this particular cliché to Tia later, for once Tia had to admit that it was very apt.

Yeung Lan went on. "It's true. Roscoe caught on very quickly according to Wu Chen and he *did* do a good job." Claire observed that Yeung Lan was addressing her remarks to the rest of them, not to Roscoe directly, and she waited nervously for what was coming next. But Roscoe understood what she was saying and smiled tentatively.

Yeung Lan went on. "Once it was clear that Roscoe was working out, Wu Heng told Wu Chen to make the work placement permanent. It was *never* Wu Chen's idea. Wu Heng explained that it was a win-win-win situation for them. Roscoe would work for less than anybody else. He was much less likely to notice any dealer interactions or unusual activities than anybody else. And best of all, hiring somebody like him would make the café look good to the police and provide great cover for their illegal activities."

Claire looked furtively at Roscoe and saw the hurt, shocked look on his face. It was obvious that he had understood a good part of what was being said. If she had those two men in front of her right now, Claire knew she would not have been able to stop herself from hitting them as hard as she could. She felt sick for this extra insult to Roscoe on top of all that he had already suffered. And she also felt helpless as to what to say to him without making the situation even worse. Daisuke pulled his chair next to Roscoe and silently put his arm around him. The look on his face was murderous and Claire thought she would not have liked to be on his bad side and meet him in a dark alley.

Daisuke cleared his throat and said, "There is one more thing. *Tell* them, Yeung Lan."

"Well, I know you people have been considering a civil suit against my husband and the café. Daisuke told me."

"Oh, n…"Jimmy started to say but Tia, sitting beside him, stepped on his foot and pinned Yeung Lan with her eyes. "Go on, Yeung Lan. You were saying?"

"Well, I wanted to make you an offer—and I think I might have done this anyway. I feel very badly for what Roscoe has been through. Chen has told me where his share of the drug money is. It is well hidden where the police are not likely to find it and that's all I'm saying about that. And Daisuke has told me how much Roscoe wanted to work in a restaurant.

"I am prepared to walk away from The Piccadilly Fish and Chip Shoppe and sell it to Roscoe for one dollar. I have prepared a bill of sale here and one or two of you can sign as witness to the transaction to make sure it cannot be contested later. I need to collect a few personal things from there but after that if I never set foot in that place again I will be happy. Wu Gen and I have enough money to make a fresh start and as soon as he finishes school we are moving. I have already put the house on the market."

Roscoe just looked at her stunned and only partially comprehending—but he was not the only one in the room who had that look on his or her face. There was a collective muttering of thanks, those present not quite knowing what to say or do. Lan pulled out the bill of sale and asked Roscoe to sign it with Fuji co-signing as his legal guardian and trustee. Then Claire and Tia both signed as witnesses to the transaction.

But Lan was not through yet. “I’m also giving you an additional $30,000.00 to make any purchases or do any renovations that are necessary to get the place going the way you want it,” she said, turning to Roscoe. Lan handed a shoebox to him containing a large collection of bills. Everyone gawked at the money and scrambled through their minds for something appropriate to say or do under the circumstances but there was nothing.

Normally, when money changes hands it’s counted but that hardly seemed appropriate in this situation. Jimmy looked at the shoebox full of wrinkled bills and thought ‘this is definitely drug money—and if we take it we will be laundering it. But he also didn’t know what to say because the money had been given to Roscoe, not him.

Chapter 50: Roscoe's Revenge

An awkward silence prevailed and people began to shuffle. Lan suddenly looked old and tired and said she would like to leave. Daisuke got up to drive her but suddenly Roscoe spoke up, "You never nice to me before. Why you give me this money and the sop now?"

Yeung Lan turned to him and said, wearily, "because you have ample grounds for a lawsuit, which I want to avoid—and also because I'm truly upset by all that has happened to you because of my family."

"O-k-a-y," Roscoe said, slowly. "The sop is mine?" Yeung Lan nodded. "The money is mine?" Yeung Lan nodded again.

After further thought, Roscoe said "I *fix* it! We have coco-cream pie everyday—and no more fish. I don' *like* fish!" He paused a moment and thought some more. "We have nice suppers, Japanese suppers—and Daisuke Ojo cook. "I not cook. Too *hard!* And I not clean bathrooms. "I hire girls to clean bathrooms—and they have to do it right or I not *pay* them. Me *owner.* Me metter…metter?" He looked at Daisuke.

"I think you mean *maître d,*' Roscoe."

"Ye-s, I *metter dee*. I tell people where they can sit. "And I wear suit—right, Jimmy?" Roscoe was referring to the wedding tuxedo that Tia had salvaged as best she could, but not good enough to return to the shop. "I get new shirt—with wuffles!"

"That sounds good, Roscoe!" Claire said brightly, and Yeung Lan had a smile on her wan face.

But Roscoe was not yet finished and Claire saw the emotion playing across his face—a strange combination of anger and glee. “And when people all happy and eating in my sop I take picture. Then I go to jail and show Wu Chen. I tell him, ‘See! This is *my* restaurant—not yours, anymore. And it is *better* than yours!’ Daisuke Ojo tell me ‘Don’ get wrong—get even.’ I *show* Wu Chen. *That* my revenge. *That* Roscoe’s revenge!”

ABOUT THE AUTHOR

In her private life, Emma and her husband, Joe Pivato, have raised three children—the youngest, Alexis, having multiple challenges. Their efforts to organize the best possible life for her have provided some of the background context for this book and others in the Claire Burke series. The society that the Pivatos have formed to support Alexis in her adult years is described at http://www.homewithinahome.com/Main.html.

Emma's other cozy mysteries in the Claire Burke series are entitled *Blind Sight Solution* and *The Crooked Knife*.

Made in the USA
Charleston, SC
15 February 2015